On The Edg

13 Short Stories

by

NOEL SPENCE

An OSWICA Publication

ISBN: 978-0-9548251-6-4
Printed by
Graham and Heslip Printers Ltd

For Heather...

Contents

GUARDIAN ANGEL

Panic started to rise in her throat. She tried her coat pockets again. It definitely wasn't there. Her purse was missing. It was gone. But how? She hadn't dropped it. She was sure of that, because she had put it carefully in the pocket of the coat before hanging it up. Another hopeless, desperate check in the pockets. Empty.

Her purse had been stolen! It was the only explanation. But how was that possible? Her eyes had been off the coat only as long as it took her to try on the new one in front of the mirror, less than a minute. There was one possible way. Someone from outside could have slid a hand inside the cubicle curtain, felt the purse in the coat, and in an instant slipped it out of the pocket.

Marianne took a deep breath and whipped open the curtain. Apart from a couple of middle aged women approaching with a red dress, the area was clear, the other changing cubicles empty and their curtains drawn back. A wave of fear washed over her. Everything was in the purse, not just her money, credit cards, debit cards, cheque card, but items of personal identity, keys, even her bus ticket.

In a strange kind of way, the theft was not a surprise. It was like a kind of culmination of the sense of anxiety and apprehension that had been growing in Marianne from the moment she stepped off the bus in the city centre. She had felt jittery, on edge, as if waiting for something bad to happen.

How could the main shopping area have changed so much, declined so rapidly? The pleasant streets and public flower basket displays had given way to pavements cluttered with traders' stalls selling bling, cheap lighters, batteries, computer accessories and fake designer clothes. The traders themselves looked like criminal types and their hoarse street vendor cries sounded aggressive, even threatening.

There seemed to be beggars everywhere, and people selling Big Issue magazines, and others wanting her to be interviewed for surveys, and spitting, swearing hoodies marauding in groups, intimidating in number and manner. In short, there was for Marianne a distinct air of menace in the city; she felt vulnerable until she was safely inside Bloomers' long-established family store. She missed David, not because he would have offered much protection or security, but simply for the company, an arm to hold on to.

Ironic then that it was in Bloomers' old-fashioned, upper-class premises that the thief or thieves had struck. Marianne found a security man and told him what had happened. He led her down a back corridor to the Office where she gave him the details and he logged the incident in a book.

"I'll call the police if you wish, miss, but it could take a bit of time and, to be honest, there's not a lot they can do. These people know where it's safe to operate. We used to have that area covered by the cameras, but some of the women customers complained until they got them removed. Best I can do is have a word with the store detectives and maybe they'll hit on some of the regular lifters."

Marianne was obliged to borrow her bus fare home from the store. She literally did not have one penny on her person. She was close to tears on the journey. It wasn't just the inconvenience the theft entailed that upset her, nor the potential financial loss; it was the feeling of being a victim, of having been preyed upon by some heartless, worthless criminal who couldn't care less what humiliation or anxiety she would suffer.

A wider worry settled on her. Everywhere she looked society seemed to be in decline. Anti-social behaviour was rife, and authority seemed unable or unwilling to do anything about it. The graffiti scrawled on the seats of the bus said it all.

How were helpless, law-abiding and civilised citizens like herself going to find justice, or ultimately survival, against the swarming forces of violence, yobbishness, lawlessness. They were so weak, so threatened. Victims.

Marianne retrieved the spare front door key from under the oil tank. Once safely inside she wanted to curl up on the couch and feel sorry for herself, but first there was the necessary business of phoning the bank and credit card companies to cancel her cards. She thought about ringing the police but couldn't bear the prospect of their invading her home with their silly notebooks and routine questions.

She was just starting her second cup of coffee when the phone made her jump. It was a woman's voice on the line.

"Hello, Miss Taylor? This is Bloomers."

"Yes?" Marianne's voice was shaking.

"We think we may have found your purse. We need you to come down to identify it."

"It's dark red, with a brass….."

"I'm sorry, but you'll have to identify it in person. Can you come to the Office. We're open late, until eight o'clock this evening, if that makes things easier for you."

"No, no, I'll come now. I'm on my way. Thank you very much."

Marianne discovered she had been holding her breath, and gave a long slow sigh of relief.

The bus ride into the city centre was in slow motion as Marianne's mind raced ahead. She tried to envisage the outcome. What was it the woman had said, that they'd found the purse? Did she mean just that, an empty purse? Surely not, she wouldn't have been asked to go to identify just an empty purse. She had heard stories, just the same, of stolen bags and purses being found a short time after the theft, dumped in toilets or litter bins, emptied of all their contents.

Maybe the thief had taken just the money and left the rest, or maybe, as the security man had suggested, the store detectives had been able to catch a well-known offender with the purse in his or her possession. It was more likely to be a woman, Marianne figured. A man would have been too conspicuous in the Ladies' Changing Room Area. She hoped she wouldn't have to meet the thief face to face, if they had caught her. She wouldn't know how to react. Would it be the store or the police or Marianne herself who would decide whether to press charges or not?

A more agreeable thought eased her mind. Perhaps some decent, honest person had found the discarded purse and handed it in. It was reassuring to think that there were still good-hearted people out there who would do the proper thing.

The central shopping area was even more crowded than before, if that were possible, with lone musicians at every corner collecting coins in their instrument cases and hats. Marianne wriggled through the noise and bustle and smells of fast food to Bloomers grand old Edwardian building, its bright red SALE posters in the windows at odds with the worn, dignified stonework.

The lady behind the desk had nails to match the window signage. She was in her fifties and there was a kindly tone in her 'Can I help you'?

"Yes, I'm Marianne Taylor. Maybe you remember me? I saw you earlier when I was in with one of the security men. I had my purse stolen from the Ladies' Changing Rooms."

"Ah, yes, here it is," replied the lady, referring to the entry she had turned to in the book. "I'm sorry about this. It's happening more and more often, sad to say."

"But you've found it. You rang me to come in and identify it."

The lady looked puzzled. "I'm sorry?"

"You rang me, or somebody did, from Bloomers, less than an hour ago. She asked me to come in here to the Office to identify my purse. I don't think it was you, the voice was different."

"I'm really sorry, but I didn't ring you, and if I didn't nobody did. There's nobody else on today, and there hasn't been a purse left in. I'm certain about that. Are you OK?"

Marianne felt a rush of blood to her face at the same time as a cold shock robbed her of breath and sent a shiver of fear right through her. She had to grab the desk to steady herself. She felt giddy, sick.

She had been tricked. It was the thief who had rung her, the thief who now had her address and house keys, the thief who right at this moment was probably plundering her lovely home. She thought she was going to faint.

The lady brought her a glass of water. What to do? Should she ring a neighbour? No good, the old couple she was friendly with would be useless. The police? But what if she was wrong, if it was just a malicious call that had been made, and nobody was burgling her house? Wasting police time, isn't that what they called it? Her brother? But he lived right on the other side of the city, he would need at least an hour to get there. No, she had to get back home as quickly as possible and see for herself.

The kind lady called her a taxi. Marianne couldn't remember much about getting into it but found herself sitting in the back giving the driver her address and telling him to hurry because her house might be getting robbed.

"Have you called the police?" he asked over his shoulder.

"No, I'm not sure if it's being done or not. It probably is, but maybe not."

The driver shook his head. He couldn't smell drink off her, but you couldn't tell what they were on nowadays. Either that, or a bit loopy.

Marianne's lip was quivering. How could anyone be so cruel, so evil? Even if they were not burgling her house, how could they make such a nasty phone call, raising her hopes and then destroying them? What pleasure or satisfaction could anyone get from doing these things to a stranger? She was about to give way to the relief of sobbing, but caught the driver's eye in his mirror and managed to control herself.

"There's a plastic bag in the back there, missus, if you're goin' to be sick."

As soon as Marianne opened her door, even before she had seen the evidence, she knew somebody had been in her house. She *felt* something different in the room. Nothing looked wrong in the lounge, but as soon as she opened the bedroom door the truth was all too clear. Every drawer had been emptied upside down on the floor, and she knew without checking that all her jewellery and valuables were gone. A terrible sickness, like some insufferable grief, took hold of her as she stared at the depredation in her own lovely private bedroom.

She knew now what victims of housebreaking meant when they said they felt like they had been personally violated. She had often heard how burglars would trash the house they had entered, vandalise it out of sheer wanton badness. She tried to comfort herself that at least she had been spared that cruelty. Something warm and wet fell on her wrist. A teardrop. A teardop of self-pity, but also of helpless rage.

Marianne knew not to touch anything. She went back into the lounge to phone the police and was just about to dial when someone knocked at the front door, two distinct raps: that grinning taxi driver had said he would wait outside to see if everything was all right. She opened the door.

She may have screamed, she couldn't be sure. Framed in the doorway, and seeming to fill all its space, was the huge form of a man, a man she recognised instantly, the terrifying individual who lived in the bungalow right opposite. A hundred thoughts rushed in a second through Marianne's panic-stricken mind. Was it he who had burgled her house? Was he behind the theft of her purse? Was he here now to finish the job, to eliminate her as a witness? Cochran. His name reached her through her terror. She was sure she was going to pass out.

"Marianne. Are you OK?"

He was speaking to her. He knew her name. Her head reeled in shock. Marianne had seen him a number of times working in his front garden, but had never spoken to him. She had noticed him watching her on several occasions from across the street as she went to and from work, and once she thought he had called a greeting of some sort, but he was such a frightening looking person that she ignored him and hurried inside. The neighbours claimed he was a former SAS man who had fought in Iraq and Afghanistan. His savagely cropped hair, facial scarring and heavily tattooed arms lent weight to their claim. Cochran was the kind of man she had gone out of her way all her life to avoid, and now here he was in her house, and he knew her name!

"Marianne, please don't be afraid. I'm not going to hurt you. I would never do that. I have brought something back for you."

Marianne discovered that she had sunk back onto the couch and had her hands over her tightly closed eyes. She opened them expecting to see a gun, or worse still, a knife, but instead saw a face, a damaged face, that was registering sympathy and solicitude.

"These are all yours," and he held something towards her in two large hands. Marianne recognised them at once, her purse, its contents, and her missing jewellery. She was too scared and confused to reply, but her face must have relaxed enough to show relief and possibly a diminution of terror. Perhaps it was the quality of his speech that diluted her fear. She may have expected, if anything, a drill sergeant's parade ground bark, but this voice was refined, educated.

"I'll leave them here on this table for you. They're safe now."

"How, where, did you get these?" she managed.

"It doesn't matter about that now. Marianne, there's something else you need to see. It means crossing to my house. Will you do that? I promise you, you will be totally safe. You've nothing to fear, from me or from anybody else."

Why should she trust him? How could she trust anybody? Maybe this whole thing was a set-up he had contrived to lure her over to his place. She had already shown herself to be naïve and gullible. All her experiences of men had proved that none of them could be trusted. Why should this brutalised-looking character from across the street be on the side of the angels?

Marianne nodded. She believed him. Incredibly, in the middle of her distress and confusion, still shaking and bewildered, she believed him.

They were outside his garage. Marianne looked back to her own house while he unlocked the up-and-over door. From this different viewpoint the familiar avenue and dwelling looked suddenly unfamiliar, strange. Misgivings almost overcame her resolve and she would have tried to run back home, but just then the door sprang up, Cochran shepherded her inside, pulled the door down into place, and she was looking at a scene she hadn't ever witnessed before, not even in crime films.

Trussed up in grotesque fashion on the concrete floor were two people, a man and a woman, both in their late teens or early twenties. Each was lying on one side with the hands tied behind the back and the feet tied together. The head was pulled back as far as it could go, and the knees were bent so that the heels were almost resting on the buttocks. What wrenched head and feet towards each other was a makeshift rope of clothes line noosed round the neck and stretched taut down the back to join the bound feet, with the hands also connected to this rope. Any straightening of the legs or movement of the hands would tighten the noose round the throat. It was an arrangement that guaranteed minimum chance of escape and maximum discomfort.

"These are the sewer rats who burgled your house and stole your property. How did they get your house keys?"

Marianne explained about the stolen purse and bogus phone call, inspecting the perpetrators as she did so. Both were typical hoodies, wearing the regulation cheap track suits, or trackies, with the hoods that gave the owners their generic name. The man's face was badly beaten, and blood was trickling out of his ear. He lay still, in sullen silence.

"So it was you, then, who tricked this lady with the phone call," said Cochran, leaning down close to the woman. "I suppose it was you who stole her purse in the first place?"

She kept a defiant silence, but fear was written all over her thin, white face. Cochran placed his foot on her throat and applied a little pressure.

"Yis, it was me, mister. Lemme go and I won't do it no more. Honest."

Marianne wondered how this low-life could have fabricated the official sounding phone call that had deceived her so easily. She felt sick. Cochran noticed her distress and suggested they go into the house to discuss the situation further. The garage had a side door which he unlocked and they entered his house at the back. He gave Marianne a glass of water and she accepted his invitation to sit down in the front room. It was clean, tidy, nicely furnished. She sipped the water and felt a little more composed.

"I want to thank you, Mr Cochran, for everything you've done for me. How did you know I needed help?"

"It's Ken." He paused, judging the moment. "I've been watching over you."

"What? What do you mean?" Marianne felt uneasy. She tried to remember if she always closed her bedroom curtains at night.

"Marianne, there's a lot of bad people out there. Very bad people. A girl like you, living on her own, is a soft target. She needs looking after, protecting. That's what I've been doing."

Suddenly some things started to make sense to her. Small things that had puzzled her. She recalled the time her bin had blown over in the storm and spilled its contents over the driveway, but next morning it was upright again with everything back inside.

So that was why he had accosted David! On their very first date David had arrived white and trembling at her door. He had been parked outside, probably combing his hair, when 'some Neanderthal' had knocked the driver's window and proceeded to give him the third degree.

"I wasn't going to argue with a psycho like that," David had pouted. "How do you exist, with Conan the Barbarian right across the street from you?"

In spite of everything that had happened, and her present situation, Marianne could hardly resist a smile. The gap between David and this man Cochran was wider than the Grand Canyon.

"Thank you," she said. "I suppose after what's happened today I could do with some looking after. How did you know I was in trouble?"

"Well, I saw you leaving and a couple of minutes later a car pulled up, down the avenue about thirty yards. They must have phoned you from the next street. She got out and knocked your door, and inside a minute he joined her and they found the right key and went in. I checked to make sure there wasn't a third one, a look-out, still in the car. They sometimes do that.

I waited until they came out, about fifteen minutes later, carrying a shopping bag. I then went out and *collected* them and brought them over to the garage for a *chat*. They had stolen the car, of course. After I had *secured* them I checked it out. Some mobile phones and other stolen items. They planned to burn the car as soon as they had finished here, and steal themselves another one."

Marianne marvelled at the easy, assured way he recounted the details. How helpless she, and most other people, would have been in the same situation.

"Tea or coffee?" he asked, and he went off to fix the coffee. Marianne looked round the room. There were several pictures of Ken Cochran and other soldiers in what looked like desert locations. She studied the freestanding framed photograph on the coffee table beside her. Colonel Ken Cochran. So this battle scarred, tattooed neighbour had been a colonel. He certainly didn't look like any colonels she had ever seen in the war films on TV.

Suddenly the strangeness of what was happening struck her. If anyone had told her a few hours ago that she would be sitting in the house opposite her own being served coffee by its fearsome occupant she would have diagnosed dementia.

"What happens now?" she asked over the coffee cup.

Cochran rolled himself a cigarette and lit it before replying. "You've got three options, as I see it. The simple one might seem calling the police and letting them take over. You want my opinion on that one?"

She nodded. "Please."

"Big mistake. First of all, the police will try to talk you out of legal proceedings. You've got your stuff back, nobody's been hurt, and it's a waste of time and money, not to mention paperwork, putting scum like this away for a few months, if they get even that. They've probably got a criminal record as long as your arm. They'll be back on the streets doing the same things as soon as they're out.

More important is what would happen to you. Your name and address would be shared around, popular currency, a well-off girl living by herself in a good area. Easy pickings. Criminals like this will do the same house time and again, regardless of what security measures the householder may take. If these two did get banged up their mates would probably take revenge, on you, your property, or both. Don't think for one moment that the police could protect you. They're overwhelmed as it is."

Marianne felt fear just listening to his appraisal. She didn't doubt for a moment that every word he said was true. He finished his cigarette and resumed.

"Option two is to let them go, and try to get back to normality. Not a chance. Don't expect natural human responses from the pair out in the garage. Scumbags like these don't know what gratitude is, or decency or compassion or any of the ordinary emotions. They would laugh at you for your softness if you let them go, and regard it as an invitation to come back for another go.

These are the rats brave young men are fighting and dying for in Afghanistan. While soldiers are tackling terrorism abroad in the name of freedom, these dregs are free all right, free to roam the streets and terrorise the decent people at home.

Next time they'll be more careful when they pay you a visit. They won't bother me. The point is, Marianne, I couldn't be sure I'd catch them every time, and who knows how they'd treat you."

He took the coffee cups back to the kitchen and rinsed them under the tap. Marianne sat still, a kind of dread on her that life was never going to be the same. And all because she had gone to buy a new coat. It wasn't fair. Why her? She wiped a tear away before he returned. He sat in the chair in front of her. She raised her head and looked steadily at him. In that rough, ravaged, masculine face she saw something totally unexpected, tenderness.

"What about the third option?" she asked. There was a long pause before he replied.

"The third one is the easiest and the most complicated. There are a lot of strings attached. It's the one I would want, but the decision is yours. You would need to think long and hard about everything involved in it, and ask yourself if it's what you want. I think you should go back over to your own house and examine what it would mean for you. You don't have to give me your answer right away, or face to face. Here's a card with my phone number, if that would be easier for you, but please, Marianne, think what comes with it. It's a commitment. You need to be sure. Like me."

Marianne had grown more nervous with every word. She couldn't speak. He waited a moment, then continued.

"Option three is to leave everything to me. I will vanish them. Completely. No more bother from them or their kind, ever. All you have to do is say the word and I'll do it......."

Vanish them. She knew what that meant all right. She had already seen the effects of his *chat* on the face of the man tied up on his garage floor.

Marianne was back in her own familiar surroundings, but instead of feeling safe she had never felt so shaky in her life. There seemed, according to Cochran, only one way to secure her future and that was to become an accessory to murder, or at least to turn a blind eye to it. She had no doubt that he could and would do what he said if she gave him the go-ahead. How many people had this man killed already in the field of war, so why would these two cause him a second thought?

And what would that mean for her? To be always under his control, his influence, for as long as he wanted. That terrible knowledge would be the secret that would bind them together in some unholy alliance until maybe he would choose to *vanish* her too.

She shuddered.

But wait a bit. He had not needed to get involved at all. He could have left her and the criminals to their own devices, kept himself out of the picture altogether. And why hadn't he? Because he was 'watching over her'. He had done everything <u>for her</u>. The tenderness in his voice and face came back to her. She shuddered again, this time with shame.

Marianne looked round her room, at all the things that were near and dear to her, and suddenly they were of no value at all. Her eye fell on the photograph of David, his handsome face studiously casual in its set, not a blemish, let alone a scar, to upset the image.

At that moment something very strange happened, something that Marianne could never afterwards find the right words to describe. It seemed that a kind of light or ray of clarity spread over and through her consciousness, a personal epiphany in which everything in her life was illuminated and evaluated. Looking back later at the experience she found an analogy in the notion that at the moment of death a man's whole life will flash before him.

She saw herself as in a vision, a moment of preternatural, heightened self-awareness:

thirty four years of age, and half of those years wasted in chasing after the kind of good-looking men who would always love themselves more than they could ever love her, or anyone else for that matter. She saw herself alone, fearful, increasingly isolated and desperate in a coarse, unfeeling world. She saw a man, a strong and good man, who would selflessly be in her life to love and protect her so that she would never again feel helpless, weak, vulnerable.

Already she was different. Stronger. She found the card that this man had given her. With completely steady hand she dialled the number, and with equally steady voice she said, "Do it."

JEALOUSY

The wind was slapping black water on the rocks as I ran through the rain the short distance from the car park to the hotel entrance. I knew I wasn't late, but an assistant Branch Manager near the bottom of the pile is overly nervous when about to meet the Managing Director presiding at the top. Not just the Managing Director, but the Founder, the Owner, the god-like person who single-handedly runs a huge global business empire in the same way as lesser men might own a sweet shop or a garage.

I had been anxious all the way up to the meeting, fearful of a puncture or some kind of mechanical breakdown, but my nervousness had started from the moment Reynolds had called me into his office and told me the Great Man wanted "to be put over" the plans and projections for our branch's proposed extension.

I had been unable to hide my surprise. "Why me? Is this not a job for you, the Manager, or at least for a managerial team?"

"I think this is one for you, Raymond," said Reynolds, with a little knowing smile that did nothing to explain his choice and only added to my uneasiness.

The news of my selection produced even more alarming commentary from others farther down the chain. They advised me that I had 'drawn the short straw' and 'won the booby prize', while Mrs Clifford on reception, the only one of us who had ever actually met Ralph Newberry in person, pronounced, "Rather you than me. He's not a nice person," in a voice that might have been telling me he had leprosy.

"It's jealousy," explained Reynolds when I mentioned these opinions to him, but again there was a kind of evasiveness in his manner that suggested things were being left unsaid.

The hotel receptionist was able to tell me that Mr Newberry was finishing his meal in the Dining Room, so I accepted her offer of a coffee in the Lounge while I waited for him. Through the heavy velvet curtains that hung down to the floor I could hear rain lashing the windows, and the slight wafting of the curtain edges revealed the power of the wind outside, but my thoughts were on the business ahead. I was confident I could field any questions or challenges about the plans in my briefcase, but I was much less comfortable about how best to deal with the man who might raise them.

Ralph Newberry was said to be one of the richest men in the country, and one of the least accessible, so what experience had I for this wholly unexpected face to face meeting in an off-season seaside hotel? I had read up on him, of course, but most of the articles seemed largely speculation and hearsay. All were agreed that he was reclusive, antisocial, parsimonious, unmarried, perhaps gay, and in his sixties, but apart from his unerring financial expertise, nothing of his professional or business life was known. He had residences all over the world, so nobody could even say for certain where the man lived.

I had made my mind up to be dynamic, assertive, and was working on the best way to open my attack, when I became aware of a figure standing just behind my armchair. I looked up and there was the Great Man himself only a yard from me.

I think it must have been the surprise and suddenness of that appearance which completely changed the direction of the whole evening, because what I saw in that first startled moment was a shy-looking, slightly stooped man who seemed reluctant to disturb my concentration.

"Newberry," he said, and had I not recognised him from a photograph, I might have thought he was asking if that was my identity.

"Nicholl," I said, standing up clumsily and catching my briefcase on its way to the floor. "Ah yes, Raymond," and I think he smiled.

Raymond. He knew my first name. Part of me was pleased that a multimillionaire should have said my name, another part was terrified that this man's thoroughness and power allowed nothing to be unknown to him, even the first name of a minnow like me.

There was an awkward silence for a moment, and then, contrary to prepared script and rehearsed role, perhaps confused and uncomfortable, or probably because some part of me wanted to, I found myself saying, "Would you like a drink?"

"Drink?" He rolled the word round in his mouth, tasted the idea. "Drink. Yes, I believe I would like a drink."

The most bizarre moment of my twenty nine years was standing there at the bar of a largely deserted coastal hotel ordering two beers for myself and for the elusive international financier, Mr Ralph Newberry. I had imagined he would have chosen an expensive brandy or rare wine, but he seemed delighted with his pint of draught beer.

His choice of drink was like a kind of symbol for the rest of the meeting. Nothing was as I had imagined it would be, especially Newberry himself. As soon as we were settled in the generous leather armchairs in front of the large open fire, he sprang the first surprise.

"Well, Raymond, are you happy with the plans for the new extension?"

"Oh yes, sir, very much."

I was about to open the briefcase and present the evidence, when he resumed, "Well, in that case we need say no more about it. I'm sure you know your job, and you wouldn't have come up here to see me if everything wasn't in order. As they say, there's no sense in keeping a dog and barking yourself."

I was completely nonplussed. What was I doing there if he didn't need to see the plans and have them explained? For an instant I remembered the rumour that he might be gay, and wondered if Reynolds and he had arranged this little out-of-the-way rendezvous, with me the unsuspecting offering to the Great One. That would explain Reynold's shiftiness. When I looked over, however, and saw the Great One with a froth moustache admiring the colour of his beer against the flare of the flames, my panic receded.

I've never liked recounting that unreal evening. People think I'm boasting, or exaggerating, or simply fabricating, but the plain truth is that, in an almost empty hotel with the wind and rain battering to get in, and the fire flickering on two men's faces, a multimillionaire and I got steadily and contentedly drunk. In the process, I got something extra, something rare and valuable, an insight into one of the most misunderstood men I have ever met or heard of or read about, a lonely man, a feared man, a frightened man. In the space of a few hours I probably learned more about him than all the reporters and commentators put together. I noted his little mannerisms, like putting his hand shyly over his mouth when he smiled, or constantly brushing his lapels with his fingers as if flicking away crumbs.

Most of our conversation was surprisingly low powered, some of it lowbrow. We talked about music, films, interests, football, but kept mostly away from private or family matters. Business wasn't touched upon at all. Unconsciously, as we graduated through gins and tonic to arcane liqueurs, I forgot that I was conversing with the almost mythical Ralph

Newberry and that I ought to be guarded in my speech.

For long periods both of us sat and enjoyed looking into the fire, happy without the need to talk. Eventually, whether through my company or the effects of the alcohol I can't be sure, he relaxed enough to talk more about himself and his private life.

He regarded his business acumen merely as something he had been born with, in the same way that some people are born with great musical or artistic gifts, or sandy hair. His attitude suggested that his financial genius put him at some kind of disadvantage.

At one point when he was explaining how people would try to befriend him purely on account of his money, and then revile him after they had failed, I was sufficiently fortified to throw in, " Jealousy. Pure jealousy." Mr Newberry made no comment.

It must have been nearing nine o'clock or thereabouts when a little incident occurred. A street urchin, a boy of nine or ten, had somehow made it into the hotel and we heard him pestering people in the adjoining Residents' Lounge for 'odds'. He had just made it over to our corner in the Main Lounge and was asking Mr Newberry, "Any odds, mister?" when a manager or some staff member came hurrying over to eject him. Mr Newberry held up his hand, reached in his pocket, and gave the ragged youngster what looked to me like a £20 note.

"Thanks, mister," and he was away in a flash, the hotel person looking at Mr Newberry as if he had lost his reason. Into my nicely lubricated mind slid some old Bible story text, "Forbid them not", or something to that effect. I couldn't but wonder how this man could have earned a reputation, along with all the others, for, of all things, miserliness.

The fire had been fed for the last time and the wind outside had strengthened so that we could hear it growling in the wide chimney. It was about an hour after the visit of the street urchin, and I was drowsily watching the firelight playing over Mr Newberry's face. His eyes were closed and I thought perhaps he had drifted off to sleep.

"You mentioned jealousy, Raymond," he abruptly said, and I jumped out of my own semi slumber. "May I tell you about jealousy, my thoughts on it? You see, I've had well over fifty years to think about it."

He closed his eyes again and for a moment I thought he had changed his mind or had dropped into an instant sleep, but then he resumed, clear-headed and steady.

" My feeling is that most people have a right to be jealous, and only a few have not. The privileged have not the right. In fact, privileged people like me must expect to be the natural targets of jealousy. That is human and understandable. What is unnatural, indefensible, is jealousy on the part of the privileged few. Their jealousy is the worst kind."

He paused. The hotel was silent except for a log shifting in the fire. I knew to wait.

"I'm going to tell you a story, Raymond, to illustrate what I've been saying. It's a story about jealousy.

Sixty years ago or so, when I was a boy of about six, an only child, I was travelling up to Scotland with my parents. They were going up grouse shooting, and I was cuddled up in the back of the big car with the rain pelting down outside. The car was warm and I could smell that lovely leathery upholstery smell that cars used to have. My dad had the radio on low, and I can remember the smell of his cigar and the roughness of the blanket I was hiding under while my mother pretended she couldn't find me. It was an enclosed little world of warmth and love in the middle of wind and wet.

Somewhere over the border we came upon a girl standing by the roadside. She wasn't hitching a ride, just standing there in the pouring rain.

My father stopped the car, reversed back, and opened the door. I can remember the cold rushing into the car, and spots of rain, and then she was in and I was staring at her. She must have been about fourteen or fifteen, and she was drenched. While dad and mum talked to her, I recoiled from her to avoid getting wet, and studied her from behind my blanket. She had dark pony-brown hair plastered over her face, and a kind of long thin cardigan wrapped round her. It was black with wetness. Her legs, purple with cold, were dripping water on to the floor of the car. She spoke in a strange way and I couldn't understand what she was saying to father and mother."

He paused again. In the leather armchair before the warm fire, and with the rain lashing down outside, he seemed to be reliving the memory.

"You know what I remember best? Her hands. She had red, thin fingers, and I noticed that her nails were very short. She had no jewellery, of course, but she had drawn a ring on one finger in ink, and the rain had made it run down on to her knuckle. The dream was there, you see."

I could see him twiddling the gold ring on the little finger of his right hand, and his voice when he next spoke was thick with regret.

"When we reached her village a few miles away and the girl was getting out of the car, my good hearted mother felt so sorry for her that she gave her a bottle of lemonade and a florin. A florin, two shillings, 10p. I saw her thin red fingers clutching the bottle, and felt an instant pang of jealousy. Why? Why should a big girl, a woman, a stranger, be given a florin and a bottle of lemonade? I wanted them. Things should be given to me. Why were my mum and dad giving presents to her instead of to me? She had no right to them. I was the one presents were given to, but my parents were choosing to give them to somebody else. I buried myself deep in the blanket and gave myself over to the dark power of jealousy....."

I don't remember much about the rest of that evening and can't even recall going to bed, but when I came down for breakfast late next morning Ralph Newberry was gone, and I never saw him again.

He had left a little note for me at Reception. I have it still. The words, written in ink that had not run, simply said: *Thank you for bringing me in out of the cold for a short time and for giving me a lift. Thank you too for the drink and for the wealth of your company. R.N.*

I wear that note against my heart. In a cold world of jealousy and misunderstanding, it is my badge of honour, my medal for service to humanity.

DEATH OF TED

On the evening of September 22nd 1958, two days after his fifteenth birthday, Danny McKenna had a life-changing experience. It wasn't a religious conversion or anything like that, although some of the effects were not dissimilar.

The source that triggered the episode couldn't have been more ordinary. It was a battered old radio whose dreary daily musical output was as familiar a part of the McKenna domestic background as the flowery yellow wallpaper that decorated the walls of the front room in which Danny was sitting pretending to do his homework.

Suddenly, without warning, without fanfare, without any of the preparation that might have been expected to accompany a life-altering moment, a sound exploded from the humble cream Cossor on the mantelpiece, a sound that set racing Danny's heart, senses, soul, his whole being, and changed his tastes and values for ever.

The sound was in the form of a driving, electrifying song delivered with an energy and rhythm that defied the listener to sit still. Danny was too spellbound to catch much of the lyrics, but someone called Johnny was being urged to behave himself, to be good. Whatever the meaning of the words, when their pulsating echo had died out Danny in some strange way felt that he had been touched to the core. He wanted to hear that sound again and again, for ever, and the loss of it, the need of it, almost brought tears to his eyes. From that moment he was on a mission, to trace that dynamic song and listen to it until his longing could be fulfilled.

His friends at school next day were no help at all in identifying the music Danny tried to describe to them, but they were agreed that if anybody would know it would be Vinty Laggan. Anything new or different or dangerous would be Laggan territory.

Danny was uncomfortable with this new direction. Laggan was a loner and had a bad reputation. He was in the special final year class set up to deal with the troublemakers, those unable or unwilling to sit exams. Danny had never spoken to him all the time he had attended school, so it was a measure of his compulsion to find an answer that he found himself seeking Laggan out at break time. Not unexpectedly, he was behind the bicycle shed having a smoke. Danny went right to it.

"Vincent, I'm Danny McKenna. I was wonderin' if you could help me find out about a song I heard on the wireless last night."

Laggan took a deep draw of his cigarette and exhaled two jets through his nostrils. "I know who y'are, all right. The undertaker's cub."

He ended there and Danny was obliged to get things back on course. "Aye, that's me. Y'see, there was a song on the wireless last night and I didn't get the name of it, but it was very fast and strong and it was about somebody called Johnny who was bad and was bein' told to be good, and that's all I can remember, but it was brilliant, really great, and I was hopin' you might know it…." The recital trailed off rather lamely.

"Nope." Laggan flicked the cigarette end away. "Sounds to me like rock 'n' roll stuff. Surprised a smart cub like you couldn't figure that out for yourself."

"No, sorry, didn't, thanks. I'd love to hear it again. Any ideas?"

Laggan allowed himself the twisted grin of one who has the right answer but knows the listener will not like hearing it. "If you want that kinda stuff, McKenna, you need to try the Acne down in Artillery Street. Watch yourself. The Teddy Boys in there have the likes of you for breakfast." The grin grew to a full-bodied sneer.

The Acne. Danny knew the place all right, but had never been in it. Its proper name was the Acme Café, but some wit had dubbed it The Acne because it was a bad spot, and the name stuck. Danny had never been expressly forbidden to go into it, as far as he knew, but he remembered his father picking him up one day in the hearse and as they drove past the café he was warned that boys who didn't do well in school would end up joining the layabouts and street corner types who frequented it.

As for the warning Laggan had given about the Teddy Boys, Danny didn't have a clue. Who were they? Had he said teddy bears? But what sense would that make? One way or another he was going to find out, because Danny had made up his mind that, whatever the risks, he was going to continue his quest….

Like most market towns its size across the country in the1950's, Ballyclifford was a drab, joyless place. Economic conditions had practically extinguished public entertainment and social enjoyment, the small Picture House and occasional dance in the Parish Hall providing what little there was.

To its credit, The Acme Café, encircled by mean houses and sandwiched between a spit and sawdust Public House and a grubby bookie's shop, managed to hint at brighter possibilities. Its owner had lived some years in America and had returned with the neon bug, the sign above his premises winking red through the prevailing grey of the district, and smaller green and blue neons glowing in the front window.

The café's deep, dark interior boasted one-arm bandits round the walls, and a table hockey game in the centre of the floor led up to the shop counter at the back, but pride of place went to the large glowing AMI jukebox that boomed and thumped tirelessly like some great engine powering the place from underneath.

Feeling self-conscious in his school uniform, and aware that he was being watched by the 'residents', Danny made his way up to the counter and ordered a Wagon Wheel and a hot orange drink. He carried his purchases over to a table and was wondering if he dare sneak a few glances round at the other customers when a small miracle happened. The jukebox made a few preparatory noises and suddenly detonated the very same musical bombshell that had touched him to the quick the previous evening. Danny would shortly be familiar with terms like *guitar riffs* and *rhythm and blues*, but for now he allowed himself simply to be enslaved by the power of the music.

Another small miracle was happening too. Everyone else in the café seemed to be similarly affected by the song, like worshippers united at the same shrine. Danny did not know who these people were, but he felt a kind of instant bonding, an affinity, a belonging, as though he had been initiated into some kind of brotherhood.

When the record ended and another began, Danny checked the devotees over the rim of his glass. They were all young men, and Danny thought he recognised a couple as having been in the leaving class his first year at secondary school. The remarkable thing was that they all looked alike, or at least dressed in a similar way, with distinctive hairstyles, clothing and footwear. The hair was combed high at the front and slicked back behind the ears at the sides, with long sideburns for good measure. As for the clothes, their dark jackets seemed too long, almost down to the knees, with velvet lapels and cuffs, and pockets trimmed with velvet too. The jackets reminded Danny of something familiar, but he couldn't quite remember what.

A few wore black waistcoats, and these few also had chosen narrow black trousers, as distinct from the tight jeans of the others. Some had very thin ties, and some wore their shirt collars raised high round the neck to prop up their greased hair, but all were united in their choice of shoes, black suede ones sitting above huge, thick soles. Danny liked the silver side buckles, and the loud socks.

These must be the Teddy Boys Laggan had warned him about, but why they had that title Danny was yet to learn. He was also to find out that everything they wore, from the drape jackets down to the crepe shoes, were being paid off in a Hire Purchase agreement with a mail order firm in Dublin. For the moment he sat back and admired the smart styles and the swagger that accompanied them.

"Are ya goin' to feed the monster, young McKenna?" came the voice behind him. The speaker was one of the couple he half remembered from school. Danny was both surprised and pleased that this sharply dressed youth with the skull and crossbones rings on his fingers should know him.

"Let's see what you're made of," the Teddy Boy continued, nodding towards the jukebox, and Danny caught on. Not only was he being invited to play a record, he was being tested. This was his initiation. His choice would make him or break him.

Danny fumbled for a coin knowing every eye was on him. His first worry was that he couldn't operate the jukebox, but once he inserted the coin and the green light came on he was clear on that round. Now the decider. And there it was, leaping out at him from the rows of title cards, *Johnny B. Goode* by Chuck Berry. Danny pressed the buttons and as the machine scanned for his selection he went back to his table, shoulders half hunched in a half swagger.

That was the birth of Danny McKenna, Teddy Boy. They ribbed him, of course, about the school uniform, and called him Altar Boy, but in an affectionate way, and the fact that Danny had money and sometimes paid for their selections on the box was no small factor in his acceptance.

The truth was that even as a schoolboy Danny was better off financially than most of the Acme Café clientele. Danny was almost unique at school in being an only child, while his classmates had unnumbered brothers and sisters. As a young child he had once asked his mother why he had no brothers or sisters.

"I was only allowed to have one," she told him, and Danny had imagined the babies being passed over a counter and some hardhearted man taking a dislike to his mother and handing her only him.

The consequences of being without siblings were not all negative, however. He enjoyed better clothes, better food, more money, and more parental attention.

Danny was smart and a quick learner, and as a daily regular to the Acne after school he soon learned the names of the artists and recordings he liked best, adding Gene Vincent, Jerry Lee Lewis and Little Richard to his selection of favourite plays. He also became familiar with the behaviour and mannerisms of his new acquaintances, noting, for example, how they would light a cigarette, take a few drags, nick it, and put it behind their ear for later.

None of this, needless to sat, was relayed to his parents. They approved of the new chess and draughts group he was attending each afternoon after school....

Anyone who joins an organisation or movement of any sort likes to wear the uniform that announces membership. It was a satisfaction denied to Danny, who every day had to watch his new associates proudly sporting their Teddy Boy gear, while he sat like the ugly duckling in his schoolwear. They in all probability enjoyed the contrast between a schoolboy's conventional clothes and their own flamboyant dress style, but Danny longed to match them in appearance. He did start to brush his hair at the front into the quiff they all seemed to favour, but recoiled from the advice they offered of combing margarine into the sides to give that sleek, oiled look.

Ironically, it was Danny's father, the unwitting barrier to his son's sartorial ambitions, who provided him with the means to satisfy them. Danny came home one afternoon just as the hearse returned from the funeral of old Ma Reynolds. As soon as his dad stepped out of the hearse Danny saw what he had known all along but had been too stupid to recognise, the potential of his coat! His long black undertaker's coat.

It wasn't this overcoat, the double breasted one, but another one, worn only on very special occasions, and unless he was wrong, it had, he didn't dare believe it, a black velvet collar! A few alterations, and he knew the very person to make them, and Danny would have a classy drape jacket equal to anything specially ordered from Dublin.

It was all too easy. At the first opportunity Danny slipped into his father's Funeral Suite, a grand name for the front parlour, dug out the coat in question from the back of the big dark wooden wardrobe that reeked of moth balls and damp, and slipped it on in front of the long mirror. Danny was a well-built boy for his age, and Joe McKenna was a slightly made man, so the coat fitted almost perfectly. The shoulders were a little wide but so much the better, matching the shoulder pads of some of the Teddy Boy drapes. What luck. What an entrance he would make to The Acne. What a stir he would cause.

The old seamstress in The Barrow had once taken in Danny's new school burberry or gabardine or something, but she gave no indication that she remembered him, asked no questions, and listened carefully as Danny gave her the instructions. He had marked with chalk the finished jacket length, fingertip, and showed her where to add the black velvet pocket flaps, lapels and cuffs. The single velvet covered button was the final touch. The woman seemed short of money and grateful for the work, and Danny left her tiny house pleasantly surprised at how little she wanted for the job.

On Friday afternoon, as arranged, Danny paid her for the finished work, smuggled it into the house, tried it on in his room, and almost shouted out with success. It was perfect. He couldn't drag himself away from the mirror, and rehearsed various poses for his grand appearance at the café on Monday after school.

At the Funeral Mass on Saturday afternoon for Station Master Martin Convery the priest delivered these words: *Here was a man who touched and influenced many lives in Ballyclifford and far beyond. Who knows how many in this parish and in this community will be deeply affected by his death, both now and in the years ahead.*

Had the priest needed to call on someone to substantiate the truth of his eulogy, he could have visited the McKenna household a couple of hours earlier when the passing of leading citizen Convery was precipitating a crisis. Like many domestic dramas, it started with a casual enquiry about a lost item, transmitted from one room to another.

"Ethy, have you seen my good overcoat, the one with the velvet collar?"

"It's in your wardrobe. Where else would it be? I suppose you want me to come and get it for you."

"If it was in my wardrobe, would I be askin' you where it is?"

It was a ritual exchange, one that always ended with the wife having to go herself to locate what her incapable man couldn't find. This time, however, there was no quick, triumphant ending. Rummagings, accusations, suspicions, memory searchings, all produced the same result, the coat was missing, and no logical reason could account for it. Ethy was almost at the point of reaching for a supernatural explanation when her more pragmatic husband asked the question that cut to the heart of the mystery---- "Where's Danny?"

The game was up. Danny, who had been listening upstairs to the growing crisis with white face and limp quiff, came meekly down with the missing garment over his arm and handed it to his father. The scene that followed was pure theatre of the absurd. Joe McKenna gravely accepted the jacket and proceeded to put it on, to a gasp of dismay from his wife and, in spite of his best efforts, a nervous snigger from his son. The three players stood in silence for a moment, as surreal a tableau as could grace any stage. Then, in the Family Funeral Suite, a redfaced angry little man with rimless glasses and a drape jacket, exorcised the demonic cult that threatened to possess the McKenna household. His words had all the authority of a Bishop: "That's the end of this, Danny McKenna, or I'll kick your arse all the way to Dublin and back......."

There's a saying among the converted, *Once a Teddy Boy, always a Teddy Boy,* and rumour has it that even today, fifty years on, there lives a successful, respected businessman not too far from Ballyclifford who, at private parties in his exclusive mansion, can be seen bopping around a large coloured jukebox and wearing strange clothes from the days of Tommy Steele and the like.....

THE TELL

Clarke waited until Burton had eased out of the station yard into a gap in the thin mid-afternoon traffic and then put the question, trying to hide his exasperation under a show of puzzled admiration.

"How did you know, sir, that he was innocent? I mean, how were you so sure from the start, when everything seemed to point to his guilt, or at least his involvement?"

Burton adjusted the driving mirror and lowered the window a fraction. True to form, he landed the question back in the server's court.

"And what exactly *seemed to point to his guilt, or at least his involvement ?*"

"Come on, sir, a man's wife disappears without trace or explanation, and he doesn't report it for nearly a week. Does that not look a bit suspicious?"

"Without explanation? There's always an explanation." Burton settled both hands on the wheel, like a speaker grasping the lectern. "When we first spoke to Williamson, you said yourself that he was hidin' somethin', and you were right, but then, who isn't hidin' somethin'? We're all hidin' somethin'. Knock on any door in this street and question the men, especially the married ones, and if you probe deep enough you'll find they're all holdin' somethin' back. Our job is to find out what."

"OK, fair enough, but Williamson didn't seem really worried about what had happened to his wife. It was like he knew already, like he was only going through the concern bit for our sake. That's why I thought there was more to it." Clarke tried not to sound too defensive.

Burton considered the analysis. "And you were right there too. Williamson didn't come to us because he wanted to, or needed to, he came because he had to. No man wants to have his marriage examined, not by the police or by anybody else, especially if it's goin' through a rocky patch and he knows he's mostly to blame for it. No, he was lookin' ahead and thinkin' how bad it would look if she came back and he had to tell her he hadn't even reported her missin'. That's why he came to us."

They drove in silence for a few minutes, Clarke sensing, as he always did, that he was being short-changed, that the senior detective was shutting him out, was putting up a smokescreen of generalisations. He couldn't let it go.

"But look, sir, a man leaves his wife to work. She doesn't come home that evening, and he doesn't hear from her for days, and he can't give us any help whatever, can't even tell us what she was wearing. Sounded a bit off to me."

"Maybe, maybe not. Tell me this, what was your wife wearin' when you got home last night? No, don't answer that, I'd have no way of knowin' if you were tellin' me the truth. Put it this way, go down the High Street right now and pick out ten married couples doin' the shoppin'. Get the men to turn their backs and then ask them what colour of coat or dress or cardigan their wife's wearin'. If you've any sense, don't put any money on them comin' up trumps."

For a man who normally said very little Burton was running off at the mouth. Anyone else might have been enjoying the moment, but Burton didn't care enough about his colleagues, or anybody for that matter, to match himself against them. Clarke tried a different tack.

"You can't say the man didn't look guilty. He couldn't look us in the eye. Real shifty, dropping his eyes all the time. Hardly the open-faced, anxious partner." Burton made the little throaty rumble that served as a laugh. "I'd have been suspicious if he had met us eye to eye. No person likes to stare another person in the face, meet a stare head on. It's not natural. Starin' straight into another man's eyes is always done deliberately, with a conscious purpose, and if a man feelin' guilty about the state of his marriage had done it to me, a stranger and a police detective, I'd have felt it was more than just a domestic disappearin' act we had on our hands."

Half an hour earlier, just at the point when the decision had been made to bring the husband in for further questioning, a decision which only Burton had opposed, the officer watching the Williamson house had rung in and reported that Mrs Williamson had returned home in a taxi and had told him under challenge that she had had to get away for a few days, to get some space, to think things through. That closed the file on the Williamson case even before it had been properly opened, and it marked yet another vindication of the instincts and talents of Detective Inspector George Burton. The only one who would not have seen it that way was Burton himself.

Clarke sat in moody silence as they drove towards the town centre. He felt he had been stonewalled yet again by his so-called partner, but then he had been warned from the start that this was likely to be the case.

"We're going to assign you to D.I. Burton," announced the Superintendent on the first day of his transfer to Barron Street. "He's our top man in the whole Division. You'll be on a winning team there." A pause. "Just a minor caution, Clarke. It's not all good news. Burton's not a team player. You'll have to watch and learn for yourself, if you catch my drift. He's not the easiest man to work with, but he's the best. Good luck."

Later another detective echoed the theme in more forthright style. "Burton's a bastard. Don't trust him and don't expect any favours from him. He dislikes everybody, and he'll despise you with your university background and your fast track promotion. He hasn't a friend in the whole Division. There's not a man in this station, from the caretaker right up to the Super, who wouldn't like to see him come a cropper. Surest way to get a medal in this place would be to bring down George Smart-Ass Burton."

Clarke's first three months in Barron Street, in fact his first three days, underlined the truth of their words. Burton told him nothing, not what he was thinking, how he was proceeding, not even where he was going, so that Clarke had to tag along and pick up what crumbs of information were left in Burton's wake. It was immensely frustrating for an ambitious young detective like Ray Clarke, the only comfort being that all the other officers knew exactly how he felt, and sympathised with him in his Invisible Man role.

"Do you play any poker at all?" Burton suddenly shot as they drove through the old, tatty town square. The question staggered Clarke, not on account of its content, but because it was literally the very first time that Burton had instigated a conversation, had opened a subject. Up to this point it had been a series of *Do this/Do that* instructions: "Wait here, follow my lead, go round the back ….."

"Poker? Some. Played a bit at school and at Training College."

Burton snorted. "I mean POKER, real poker, not your piddlin' penny-Annie stuff. I'm talkin' about the heavy sort, where a wrong call will cost you a grand or more. Have you been there at all?"

Clarke conceded that he had only seen poker at that level in films or on TV, that those stakes would have been too rich for his pocket or his knowledge of the game.

"Let me tell you somethin', and believe what I'm sayin': if you want to be up there with the great detectives, the real crime-solvers, it's not college or university you need to attend, it's Poker School. That's where you'll learn the business. All that stuff they told you at the Academy is fine as far as it goes: take the statements, get the leads, follow the facts, gather the evidence, find the witnesses, build the case, all that malarkey is grand, but look at the crime figures today, the detection rates, the conviction tables, and tell me if they're good enough to worry the criminals out there on our streets."

Clarke sat afraid to speak in case he interrupted this extraordinary outpouring. Burton had never been this expansive before, not with him and, he was sure, not with anyone else. He felt himself present at an unprecedented and perhaps never-to-be-repeated revelation. Burton was continuing.

"Crimes are human behaviour, acts committed by people, some of them bad people, some not so bad, some not bad at all, but all of them people, and to understand crime you have to be able to read people. That's what it comes down to. That's what I learned from years of playin' serious poker, how to read people. It's the hardest thing in the world to do, to read other people, but when you learn it you have the measure of even the cleverest criminals in the book."

Clarke felt he could safely reply. "Yes sir, we were taught interrogation techniques and interview methods. We had hours, days, of training, questioning suspects, cross examining, sweet and sour, role play, all the best practice."

Burton snorted again. "Best practice. No doubt that included spottin' the tell-tale signs. Like Williamson droppin' his eyes, not lookin' us straight in the face. I know the stuff you were told: the suspect swallowin' too much, or yawnin', coughin', swearin', shoutin', sniffin', sweatin', stammerin', or repeatin' himself, or his leg shakin' below the table, or scratchin' his head, blinkin' too much, holdin' his hand over his mouth, twiddlin' his weddin' ring. You know what these are? These are normal signs of nervousness, just as likely to come from a totally innocent man as from a villain. In fact, more likely to come from an innocent man than from a villain.

But every man does have a tell. That's what the good detective does, he finds the real tell, the deep-down personal, individual giveaway, and ignores the simple nervous reactions that can make an innocent man look guilty. Find the tell and you know your man." Clarke was intrigued, both by what he was hearing and by the fact that he was hearing it at all. He felt special, privileged, that he was the one, probably the first one, the only one, that Burton had communicated with in this way. He must have created a good impression to date, shown real promise, that Burton had seen fit to confide some of his methods to him. He was sufficiently emboldened to look for more.

"What are these real tells, sir? I mean, how do you know when you've seen one?"

"Ah," Burton laughed, "that's the million dollar question. There's no easy answer to that one. Each man has his own private tell, there's no general rule. Experience will teach you to spot it. Best I can do is give you an instance. You remember Dougan, the embezzler we put away the first week you were here? A bad bit of work, a real mean one. I spotted his tell all right. Whenever he was put under hard pressure, in danger of bein' cornered, he started to use big words, the kind of words he would never ordinarily use. *Comprehend* instead of *understand, conception* instead of *idea,* that kind of thing. Sometimes people do this, of course, for other reasons, but in his case it only happened when he was in a really tight squeeze. It was his support, his bolt hole. It was also his tell."

If Clarke hoped that this intimate conversation would mark a thaw in the working relationship between his superior officer and himself, he was immediately set to rights next day when Burton went back to his former ways, dour, uncommunicative, secretive. The whole episode was like an aberration he wanted to forget, and, if anything, the distance between the two men widened in their daily professional dealings. Clarke said nothing about it to the other men in the station, even though he knew they would have been more than interested. His gut feeling was to keep the conversation to himself.

Six weeks after the Williamson business, Burton had arranged to pick Clarke up one morning at the corner of his avenue. As soon as the vehicle, one of Barron Street's seven unmarked police cars, came into view Clarke saw that the passenger side was badly damaged, the front door showing a serious dent, and a deep scrape, or gouge, running the full length of the side.

Burton motioned to him to get into the back seat, the front passenger door clearly out of operation.

"What happened, sir?"

Burton twisted the driving mirror so that he could see his rear seat passenger. After a long pause he said, slowly and steadily, "I'm not a man who trusts anybody. You should know that by now. All I'm goin' to say is that no other vehicle was involved and nobody was injured. That makes two of us now who know the facts. If anybody else gets to know them I'm goin' to know where it came from, and I won't be pleased."

With that, Burton rearranged the mirror and drove in silence to Barron Street, Clarke feeling like a fare in the back of a taxi. Burton parked the damaged car in his usual place and they walked together into the Edwardian building that had originally been a hospital, and still showed its cream and green tiled walls to prove it.

Burton got the Accidents Book from Blake on the desk, and started writing his report in it.

"Bit of a scrape, sir?" asked the nosey Desk Sergeant, the broadcaster of most of the rumours and gossip that echoed every day round the rooms of the old-fashioned station.

"It's a warning not to go to these All Night Shopping Centres. What you save on the Special Offers, you put towards repairing the damage done by the boy racers. Don't worry, I'll be round there this morning checking the security cameras."

Had Clarke not been involved in the matter he might well have missed them, but, interested to hear what story Burton was going to give and perhaps alert for any weakness, he picked them up right away; the INGS; *warning, shopping, repairing, morning, checking.* They rang out from Burton's mouth like alarm bells. Clarke had never once before heard an 'ing' ending from Burton, and now he felt a kind of thrill in believing he had spotted a chink in the armour of the master detective. What Burton could detect in others who were lying or under pressure he had involuntarily betrayed in himself, a TELL.

Again Clarke's instinct was to keep the theory to himself. Something told him that sooner or later he might need it, might be able to use it.

Clarke hoped for some confirmation of his discovery and he didn't have long to wait. Just a week or so later Burton and he were on their way to investigate a major theft. Clarke was looking out the car window, having failed to get a hold on his superior officer's thinking or approach to the case, when Burton suddenly announced, "I'll not be in work for the next couple of days."

Clarke judged it proper to show concern. "Is everything OK, sir?"

"D'you like Dylan?" came the reply. "I was a great fan of his early stuff. Too early for you, I suppose. Some great songs. I was never much of a singer myself, but I used to have a go at this one:

Don't ask me no questions
And I'll tell you no lies.

Yep, that was a good one, all right."

Clarke went back to looking out the window.

Clarke and Burton were back in tandem as usual on Thursday morning. Burton made no reference to his two days' absence, and Clarke knew better than to mention it. Blake was again on duty. The man was amazing. He was like a fixed feature, almost a kind of institution. He seemed to be permanently on duty, preferring work to 'the home situation'. It was claimed he did double shifts and other people's overtime free of charge in case he missed any news or tittle tattle. Anything Blake didn't know about station goings-on hadn't yet happened.

"All well, sir," he called over to Burton. It was Blake's favourite phrase, and he had the delivery perfect, so that it could either be a statement that everything was in order, or an enquiry about things in general, or about someone in particular. Burton went for the third option.

"Yes, thanks, Blake. Having a little bit of bother with the waterworks. Had to get the old plumbing checked out. It's good for a few more years, they tell me."

Smart, Clarke thought. Telling Blake the lie was as good as putting it on the Evening News. What Burton had actually been doing, where he had really been, what the true reason for his time off might be, and why he chose to lie about it, these were matters nobody but Clarke would be wondering about......

The sequence of events that followed shortly afterwards began in a way that with anyone else would have seemed casual, normal, but when Burton suddenly declared, "I'm thirsty. D'you fancy a pint?" Clarke was so surprised that he couldn't be sure if he replied or not. Next thing Burton had pulled up at The Barking Cat, a fairly rundown place near the river, and one as contradictory as its name in its ability to attract business and even professional customers. Bar food smells lingered from the lunch period as the two men, almost by instinct, chose a table from where they could see the pub entrance and the comings and goings.

"I'll get these, sir," offered Clarke, but Burton asked what he was having and made his way to the bar. Clarke watched his boss ordering the drinks. He was wondering if he was breaking new ground in having a pint with his notoriously solitary and unsociable boss when he noticed that Burton was in conversation with a man seated by himself at the end of the bar counter. Their body language suggested they knew each other, that this was no casual chat. It immediately occurred to Clarke that what he was seeing was an arranged meeting, that there was nothing random about the invitation for a drink or the choice of pub. He should have known it. Burton would never have a drink for its own sake, there would have to be an ulterior reason.

Clarke felt a bit foolish for believing he had been asked simply to go for a pint. Just then his eye caught a slight movement below counter level and he clearly saw the man pass what looked like a small package or envelope to Burton. The transaction was quick and practised and Clarke was certain that it was one that had been done a number of times before.

"Everything OK, sir?" he asked when Burton brought over the two dripping pints, setting them down at the same time as the man left by the side entrance.

"Fine, Clarke, fine. I was just having a word there with an old colleague, one of the best. Living down this way now. Off the force. Good copper. Heart trouble."

How transparent the lie seemed. What was it Burton had said, "Find the tell and you know your man." Clarke felt a little shiver of excitement, or fear, or satisfaction, he didn't know which, but it was a good feeling, the feeling of being in control…

Blake was the first port of call. As soon as Burton had gone off duty that evening and driven out of the yard, Clarke made his way to the front desk and engaged the desk sergeant in small talk. He quickly got to it.

"Sergeant, you're the very man might be able to help me out. I called into The Barking Cat last night for a pint and got talking to this guy at the bar. Said he used to be in uniform, but had to come out with a heart problem. Big guy, with a long thin face. In his fifties, I'd say. Asked me to give his regards to George Burton, but there's the problem. You won't believe it, I just can't remember his name. It's right there on the tip of my tongue, but I just can't get it. I must be slipping up. Blame the drink! I daren't mention it to Burton without knowing the guy's name. Ring any bells?"

As he expected, Blake knew nobody fitting the description. Clarke came away without a name but with a growing conviction that he was on to something. He had an excellent eye and memory for faces, and twenty minutes of looking through the photo file of the local villains did the business. There he was, the man at the end of the bar, Lionel Alfred Davis. L.A.D.

Clarke next checked the man's criminal record. He was a bit of a lad all right, with a lengthy record going back thirty odd years and covering all the popular brands of dishonesty: fraud, theft, receiving, forgery and the like. He had done several short spells inside. Clarke examined the most recent entry in the file. Davis had been questioned about a counterfeit passport racket but had been released without charge through insufficient evidence. The Investigating Officer had been D.I. George Burton.

So this was his boss's 'old colleague, one of the best, good copper'. There could be only one explanation for the lie: Burton was bent, he was on the take.

Clarke called in at The Barking Cat on his way home. He was good at his job. A veiled threat to the owner about the legality of the gaming machines on the premises, and a few quid to the lugubrious barman, and he came away with what he wanted, confirmation that Burton and Davis had met there before, at least three times.

When Clarke came later to look back on his own conduct he was honest enough to admit that he could not represent himself as blameless. What he could claim in his defence was that working every day with D.I. Burton had rubbed off on him, changed his working practices. Where once he would have talked an investigation over with colleagues, tested his theories with other professionals, he now kept things to himself, kept his cards close to his chest. In this particular case his fellow officers would no doubt have urged him to proceed with great caution, or possibly even abandon the idea altogether.

But Clarke had ambitions. He knew the Super had once headed up an Enquiry Team into police corruption, that it was his pet hobby-horse. He was also confident that the rest of the men in the station, of every rank, would approve of a fellow officer being shopped as long as that officer was George Burton. Never once had he heard anyone try to defend Burton or even make allowances for him. Anyhow, he told himself, it was his duty....

Clarke took a deep breath and knocked. He hadn't had any direct face to face contact with the Super since his opening day at Barron Street.

"Ah, Clarke. Come on in. You're well settled in, I hear. How long is it now?" He didn't wait for an answer. "And how are you getting on with D.I. Burton?"

Clarke hesitated. "Well, sir, it's actually D.I. Burton I've come to see you about."

The Super gave a barely perceptible little nod, as though he had been almost waiting for this development. "Not working out between you?"

"It's not that, sir. I've no complaints there." A serious pause. "Sir, I have to tell you I think D.I. Burton is on the take. I've reason to believe he's not straight."

Clarke thought the silence that followed was going to go on for ever. The Superintendent's face was inscrutable, but it was clear that he hadn't been prepared for this turn of events. When he finally spoke, each word was heavy with implication.

"That's a serious allegation, D.C. Clarke, a very serious allegation. I know you must have thought long and hard about it. It's at my desk now and it's going to be investigated thoroughly, you have my word on that. What I need from you is a full report together with all the evidence. I'm on my way out to a Conference now, but see me at eleven tomorrow morning. Have you mentioned your suspicions to anyone else?"

"No sir, nobody."

"Good. Keep it that way. Tomorrow at eleven."

Clarke busied himself with case files for the rest of the day and managed to stay out of Burton's way. About half four he was returning some of the files when Burton appeared from one of the Interview Rooms. He was rubbing his hands together in satisfaction, and seemed to be in unusually good mood.

"Clarke. The very man I was thinkin' about."

"Me, sir? Hope it was good," replied Clarke, feeling uneasy.

"Just netted another one," said Burton, indicating the Interview Room with his thumb. "Nelson, our 'Cars Stolen To Order' specialist. Got his tell and his game was up. It reminded me to finish tellin' you about the power of poker trainin'. Remember?"

"Yes, sir."

Burton nodded an invitation and Clarke followed him into what he called his den, a room differentiated from the others by the disarray of its contents. For a man careful about everything he said and did, Burton had no sense of material tidiness or order, and Clarke sometimes wondered what the rooms in his house must be like.

"Yes, never did get round to completin' the poker story. It's worth listenin' to, if you've got a minute. Let me tell you about the best poker player I ever met, the one I've modelled myself on. He took the tell to a higher level.

This guy knew every move he made was bein' watched, studied, so he counterfeited a tell, made one up. It was the faintest little flarin' of the nostrils, but the boyos he was playin' with noticed it all right. Two big hands in a row he would show the tell, and lose both games when they called his bluff. Third time he showed the tell there was big money goin' down, real big money, and that's when he would spring the trap and clean up the opposition."

Clarke felt a kind of chill starting to creep over him. He knew he was being told something important, but wasn't sure exactly what. Something in Burton's story had a particular relevance for him, Clarke could feel it in his very being.

"Think about it, Clarke. The value of the tell, and better still, the value of the false tell. Making the truth sound like a lie. The uses it can be put to. Nearly as good as having a snitch. Oh, give my regards to the Super if you're talking to him. See you tomorrow."

A terrible pounding had started in Clarke. He wasn't clear if it was in his head or chest. He swallowed hard, made sure Burton was gone, and rushed up to the Entrance area. A panic grabbed him when he saw Blake wasn't on the desk, but his replacement said he was having a cuppa in the canteen. Clarke found him at a table on his own, and managed to compose himself enough to chat about other things before cutting to the chase.

"By the way, Sergeant, you remember my boss got his car damaged at that Late Night Shopping Centre? Did we ever pick anybody up for that?"

Blake growled a laugh. "So Burton didn't tell you? He's a close one, and no mistake. Good as his word, he picked the two lads out on camera, clear as a bell. Might as well not have bothered, all they got was a few weeks' community service."

Clarke fought down a rush of cold fear in his stomach. "Aye, you're right, he's a close one for sure. Didn't even tell me he was going in for a check-up. Did you know already before you asked him?"

Blake growled again. "There's not much gets by me. Heard it from Glover from Traffic. His wife's a sister on the men's waterworks ward."

Clarke's knees were rubber. He took a seat beside Blake and took the blindfold off to face the death blow. "Who's this Lionel Arthur Davis Burton meets from time to time?"

Blake looked sharply at him. "So you know about Davis? I'm surprised Burton let that slip. That's not like him. He's very careful about his snitches. Doesn't share them. Protects them. Even I'm not supposed to know about Davis. Some things you don't know about, sir, or don't talk about, and snitches is one of them. No, you don't talk about snitches."

Clarke felt his head whirling. Next morning at eleven o'clock he had to meet with the Super with a full report on a very serious allegation that was based on nothing more than poker games and false 'ing-ending tells.......

PUFFED OUT

With a clarity that thirteen years had failed to obscure, Robbie's first attempt at smoking came back to him. He was thirteen and was being tutored by an expert, little Luigi Salandini, the barber's son, who seemed to have been born with a cigarette in his hand. The setting was propitious too, the public park on their way home from school, but the experience was less than satisfactory.

"Just take a puff and inhale," prompted Luigi.

Robbie wasn't sure how to inhale, so he held the smoke in his mouth until it started to taste bitter on his tongue, and then swallowed it. The effect was instant, a lightness in the head like he had stood up too quickly, followed by a kind of sickness. There and then Robbie decided that smoking was not for him. The only pleasant thing about the whole experience was the nice tobacco smell that lingered on his fingers for a couple of days.

Now here he was again, thirteen years later, with another cigarette held awkwardly between his fingers, as in some kind of weird periodical experiment. This time, however, the motive was not curiosity or peer pressure, and there was no failure option.

It was only the previous day that he had happened to remark to Gerry Breen that he was becoming disillusioned with the job, felt he was being overlooked, taken for granted, while those with lesser claims were getting any recognition or promotion that was on offer. Gerry listened from behind his Marketing Manager's desk.

"You're not in the club, Robbie. You have to be a fully paid up member." Breen gave a little knowing laugh that said he was a member of this mysterious club.

"What club? What are you talking about?" Robbie couldn't disguise the note of resentment that accompanied his curiosity.

"The Smokers' Club, old son. That's where the top people meet. That's where the decisions are made. You're a bit slow on the uptake, Robbie, if you don't mind me saying so. Haven't you noticed that all the people going places in this company are in the Smokers' Union, the Tobacco Brotherhood?"

No, of course he hadn't noticed. It wasn't that Robbie was short on the smarts, it was simply that until he had got married to Sylvia he had been without ambition and interest in work prospects. Now, with the arrival of new responsibilities in the form of mortgage repayments and unending bills through the letterbox, he was increasingly aware of the world of salary scales, increments, job opportunities, wage increases. This awareness was sharpened by consistently unfavourable comparisons Sylvia made between their financial situation and that of their friends. She didn't exactly complain; it was more a case of, "I wish we could afford the carpet Dean and Susie have in their lounge," or, "I wish we could go away for a weekend break, the way Elliott and Rachel do." Robbie began to feel less than adequate as husband and provider....

The walls of the Smoking Room had probably been white originally, but they now wore the same nicotine tan as stained the fingers of its regulars. These were indeed, as Breen had indicated, the 'top people', together with thrusting younger staff already started up the company ladder.

They were initially surprised to see Robbie, but quickly welcomed him through the haze and didn't seem to suspect for a moment that he was a raw beginner, an impostor. Robbie had bought his packet of cigarettes and box of matches on his way to work. He was surprised how much they had cost. He had told Sylvia of his plan, of course, and her pretty mouth had instantly assumed the same primness it had shown when she had persuaded him early in their engagement to give up his two nights' rugby training each week.

" The whole thing sounds like a stupid idea to me. I hate cigarettes, Robert, you know that. Your clothes will reek of tobacco, it'll make me sick. How long do you intend going on with this? There'll be no smoking in the house, let's get that straight...."

He was careful to have the cellophane off the packet in advance in case his clumsiness betrayed him. With slightly trembling fingers Robbie put the tipped end between his lips, struck a match, and lit the cigarette. He somehow imagined the others would be watching him, assessing his performance, evaluating his worthiness as a member, but nobody was paying him any regard, not even Gerry Breen, who was gabbling away with his fag professionally held in his mouth.

There again was that same unpleasant taste, bitter and burning, but Robbie knew enough now to inhale the smoke and even bring some down his nostrils. Coughing or choking had been a worry, but neither happened. His eyes were already watery-sore from the atmosphere in the room, so they weren't a giveaway. Robbie blew out the excess smoke and, emboldened, took another draw. His head did indeed feel light, but among the various sensations he was feeling there was an almost pleasant little kick, not unlike the one he sometimes got from a cup of good coffee. Robbie finished his cigarette and to underscore his triumph lit a second a few minutes later in the middle of a conversation with one of the junior managers.

The first thing he noticed that evening when he got home from work was one of those novelty public notices propped up on the mantelpiece: NO SMOKING! SOME OF US ARE TRYING TO BREATHE. He laughed dutifully and told Sylvia of his success in the Smoking Room, but she was more concerned about the tobacco smell infecting the house, and about Robert getting hooked on the awful things......

How right she proved to be. Robbie's nicotine addiction was insidious but extraordinarily rapid. At first he smoked only a couple of cigarettes a day, always at set times and in the Smoking Room, but one lunchtime a few of them went out to The Silver Swan to toast a colleague's fortieth, and later Robbie was surprised to discover that he had smoked 8 cigarettes. He had to buy an extra packet.

Without knowing exactly how or when it started, Robbie began thinking of the cigarettes in his pocket, and even found himself involuntarily reaching for them. Soon a cup of coffee, or a pint at the Swan, was incomplete without a smoke to go with it. Robbie really did enjoy the whole smoking experience. He bought himself an expensive silver lighter which he managed to keep hidden from Sylvia. What he couldn't hide from his wife was the fact that he now wanted, or needed, to smoke outside of the workplace, something he did in the garden, or in the garage or garden shed if it was raining.

Sylvia's opposition might have been stronger had it not been that Breen's advice paid off. Robbie through the Smoking Room route quickly got to be on good terms with some of the people who mattered in the promotion game, and was raised to a Supervisor's role that brought with it an additional two hundred a month. A mere ten months later an opening arose for a Dispatch Manager and Robbie got a whisper through the smoke that he should apply. To celebrate this second promotion Sylvia and he finally managed the new curtains she had been wishing for, and topped them off with a 'weekend away'.

It was Mr Roland's nephew from London who arrived to run the business when the great old founder member of the company dropped dead one wet Saturday morning from a massive heart attack. Denis Broderick was one of those people who go right through life without ever asking themselves, even once, if they could possibly be wrong about anything. Robbie disliked him on sight, his flaky scalp, weak chin, and reedy but peremptory voice.

Broderick immediately set about making changes, more because he knew he could than perceived he should. "There'll be no dead wood in this building," he was heard to declaim on the morning of his arrival. One of the very first victims of the New Order was the Smoking Room, which overnight became an Executive Suite. Nobody knew exactly what an Executive Suite was, or did, but that was what it said on the door, and who could argue.

The former inmates of the Smoking Room were relegated to the street outside the front door, and shortly afterwards were denied even that. Broderick announced that it gave a bad impression to have staff huddling around the main entrance blowing smoke at passers-by, and added that if anyone insisted on going on killing themselves, they would have to confine themselves to the back yard, and only at lunch time.

It quickly became clear that not only were the smoking fraternity no longer in a privileged position, but that the situation had been reversed to such an extent that it was positively detrimental to their standing and prospects to continue the practice. Broderick was known to frown upon the activities of the Smoking Club in the back yard, and as a consequence its numbers dwindled until only a handful of diehards kept the tradition going. Ironically, Robbie, the last member to be enrolled, was one of the Five Pack, as they came to be known.

The new ethos at work produced further effects for the smokers. When the weather hardened into a frosty autumn, they decided the back yard was bad for their health, and took to slipping down to the local at lunch time. A couple of pints accompanied their sandwiches and cigarettes as they defiantly denounced 'Despot Denis', who, in the words of one of the hotheads, had 'endangered their health and ruined their quality of life'......

Robbie sat heavy- breathing over his pint. They were sitting in the big bow window area of The Silver Swan, the air heavy with smoke. Outside a bright March midday sun lit the brightly coloured barges moored all along this stretch of river, and glinted on the roofs of the cars in the pub car park, but Robbie's mood was dark.

Sylvia and he had had yet another disagreement. They were always disagreements, never rows, although Robbie would have much preferred a blazing stand-up shouting match. Instead it followed the standard pattern, with Sylvia lamenting the losses incurred in her marriage, and he lamely defending himself against her powder puff complaints.

"I wish you could see yourself, Robert, and what has become of you. I'm sorry for you. I wish you were the Robert I married, fit and healthy and active. If only I could get the old Robert back, the one who wasn't nearly 17 stone, who enjoyed sport, and who didn't smell of drink and cigarettes. The one who didn't slouch about taking no interest in anything, not even me. The one who...."

And so it went, her wish list a swollen volume of regrets. Robbie stubbed out his cigarette and was raising his glass to his lips when something white caught his eye on the towpath outside the window.

A group of joggers in shining white corporate tracksuits was threading its way along the well-worn track. At one time Robbie himself might have been on a similar training run, but nowadays he avoided exercise of any type. He was just about to return his attention to his pint when something about the leading joggers froze the glass in its mid-air passage. At the head of the straggling line of joggers was Mr Denis Broderick. Right on his shoulder, as though pushing for position, was a pink and athletic Gerry Breen, exhaling puffs of warm breath into the cold, bright air....

OUR PLEASANT VICES

The gods are just and of our pleasant
vices make instruments to plague us.
(Shakespeare)

It had been so long since Wesley had rubbed his hands together with satisfaction that he started wrongly and had to rotate them and turn them over to get the movement right. Old and new too for him was a pulsing excitement in his very being, a feeling he could have described only as a mental tingling.

They were safely checked in to the hotel as Mr and Mrs Green. Lorraine was having a shower to wash off the phantom dust of the journey, and he had come down to the bar for a drink. Wesley was not normally a whisky drinker, but it was whisky he chose now, a kind of gesture of continuity.

'A drop of the softest hard stuff with just a whisper of water in it' was what he had taken three weeks earlier when he had arrived in work with streaming eyes, peppery nose and swollen throat. The remedy had been prescribed and administered by Charles the accountant who was known to have a bottle permanently on his person or in his desk.

"Take a sup of that, Wesley. It might do you no good at all, but it'll make you feel better."

Amazingly, it did both. Out of professional sympathy with his patient Charles undertook to share with him in taking the medicine, and together the two of them put away the best part of the bottle.

Someone else was sharing in the office that morning; old McCrae had chosen to give selected readings from his morning paper to a less than receptive audience.

" *Bed and Breakfast, Evening Meal and a bottle of wine, for two people, for only £80. The Abbeydene Hotel, Stipsel.*"

"Stipsel? Wear the fox hat."

"*Modern comfort and facilities in an old world setting,*" McCrae continued, ignoring the sniggering, "*Privacy and Service. A Getaway Treat at a Giveaway Price.* Sounds to me too good to be true."

"Sounds to me like just the place for a dirty weekend."

"What was that name you said? Stipsel? Never heard of it. Who would go to some backwater like that?"

"I would," said Wesley, beaming and steaming from his medication, "if I had someone to go with me."

This was unexpected and produced a round of laughter. Wesley was the quiet, reserved one, and they recognised the effects of the 'medicine' in his volunteering. Wesley too knew that it was the whisky that was talking, that without it he would have been a background listener.

When he came back after lunch, still a little giddy, not fully in control, Wesley saw a folded note on his desk. Its message was clear and direct.

I'd go with you.   Lorraine.

He stared at the words like a man might stare at a stick of high explosive sitting on his dinner plate. Was he drunk and imagining things? No, it was real, undeniable, unignorable. Taking a deep breath he raised his head and looked up to the top end of the large room. There she was, steadily watching him, watching and waiting. There was no smile or playful wave or anything to suggest that she was having a joke. The next play was his.......

Propped on the bar stool, Wesley took a sip of his whisky and smiled to himself. He had played it well, very well, if he might say so. Up to that morning Lorraine Green, the woman now upstairs having a shower in THEIR room, had been someone in the office he would nod to, or exchange the usual pleasantries with. He knew virtually nothing about her beyond her being a widow and there being some kind of cloud or mystery or something connected with her. Whatever it was, nobody talked about it. She was in her late thirties, he reckoned, slightly plump, and with wavy fair hair. He had never thought of her as anything more than a fairly nondescript colleague.

Wesley's return of serve was to take his mobile phone up to the flat roof where the exiled smokers had congregated at first until the Health and Safety boys had put a stop to it. She lifted her phone immediately.

"This is Wesley. Are you serious?"

"Totally. Are you?"

As soon as he realised Lorraine was for real he wanted her, had to have her. He felt a dryness in his mouth and a strange tugging in his stomach. "Yes, I'm serious." Pause. "What do we do now?"

In fairness, Wesley had to acknowledge that most of the 'logistics' of the thing were handled by Lorraine. She booked their night at the hotel on-line, used her card to pay the deposit, and planned the route they would take to Stipsel. He marvelled at the cool way she behaved in the office, cool because it was exactly the same as always, without a flicker of anything at all between them. Who could have imagined that the quiet woman seated at the desk near the coffee machine was capable of such secret thoughts and plans and desires.

Wesley's job was to doublecheck the plan for weaknesses and to come up with a story that would convince his wife. He made Lorraine take two days off, the Thursday as well as the Friday; someone in the office might be suspicious if they were both off on the same day. He also arranged to pick her up from a railway station car park eight miles south of town, the direction they were heading, in case they were seen together driving across town. All their communications were from one mobile to the other, at lunch time, outside the building. Wesley insisted they should not meet or be seen talking together.

All this was easy, of course. The big one was getting past Eleanor. Not that she had any reason to mistrust him or suspect anything, but Wesley thought it best to assume suspicion and be ready for it. She was away from home far more often than he had ever been; it was the infrequency of his away nights that necessitated careful explanation for this one. He settled for a Trade Show, having been at one shortly after they were married. He remembered they had met at it for lunch.

It was easier than he could have hoped for. He came home in an affected grump.

"Eleanor, you'll never guess, those idiots on the top floor want somebody to attend a Trade Show the Friday after next down in Silverton, and who d'you think they've picked to go?

Muggins here. It's because I'd been at one years ago, or maybe it's because nobody else would agree to go. It's daft, crazy." He was careful to steal any ammunition she might have used. "I mean, this is the age of the catalogue, the Internet, the browsing and shopping on-line. What do they need me there in person for? I allowed myself to be talked into it, but I've a good mind to go in there tomorrow and tell them to find some other softie." "Don't be silly, Wesley. You should be flattered they chose you to go. Have you to stay overnight?"

"Yes," sulked Wesley, "and you know I hate being away from home. I never sleep properly. The whole thing's a waste of time."

He almost protested too much. "Well, don't go if you don't want to. They'll find somebody else."

"Only thing is," Wesley came in quickly, "I'd make a killing on the travel expenses. A 300 mile round trip at 40p a mile. What's that, a hundred and twenty quid! I suppose I could take my Nytol."

Eleanor laughed and kissed him on the cheek. She sometimes seemed to regard him as a wayward child who ought not to be taken too seriously.….

Wesley smiled, thought about another whisky, and instead ordered his usual, a gin and tonic. He rang home on his mobile. Eleanor was out, but he left a message that he was safely arrived in Silverton and the hotel was grand. His mind drifted upstairs to Lorraine. He could hardly believe that he was about to spend the night with a woman he had seen every day for about twelve years, and had never taken seriously under his notice until the last twenty days or so. Now he could hardly wait to be with her.

The whole thing was like a game, a ritual. Both were longing for each other, each knew it, but somehow the delaying, the dalliance, was part of the pleasure. They were like two Sumo wrestlers who observe all the niceties and protocol of the sport while knowing that these inevitably precede an explosive coming together.

The game was under way from the moment Lorraine slid into the passenger seat beside him in the car park. She had her hair up in a French pleat, wore red dangling earrings, and exuded a perfume so alluring that Wesley felt almost intoxicated by it. In contrast her manner was controlled, and their conversation was artificial, studied.

Wesley unintentionally broke through the wall early, something that was undoubtedly going to happen sooner or later. "I'm not very good at all at this kind of thing. This is my first time."

His honesty was the key that unlocked Lorraine to him. "Snap. Can you believe that this is the first time I've been alone with a man for over ten years?" She paused, looked across at him, and continued. " Just getting ready to go out to meet someone, choosing what to wear, and the make-up and even the packing, I can hardly believe it's happening. Honestly, if you were to change your mind right now and stop the car and put me out, it would still be worth it just for the enjoyment of being alive again, even for the last few hours."

Wesley wasn't sure how to react. "So it wasn't me in particular, then? Any man would have done?"

She looked hurt. "Wesley, you are the only man in that office, in that whole building, that I would have given that note to. I may be lonely, maybe even desperately lonely, but I'm not a tramp. I've been watching you for months, years, but you never noticed me. I've been going out with you in my mind for as long as I can remember."

Wesley felt he had to offer some kind of explanation. "I'd no idea, none at all. It's just that.....there seemed to be some kind of.....something about you, as if people were afraid of saying something that would damage you. I don't know how to put it. We were worried about saying the wrong thing, or something like that, it's hard to put into words."

She told him the whole story, evenly and with surprising detachment. Two years after their marriage her husband was killed late one night in a car smash, but the tragedy didn't end there. Also killed in the accident was the woman he was having an affair with, Lorraine's best friend, chief bridesmaid at her wedding. The trauma and emotional repercussions were enough to leave Lorraine in a fragile nervous condition that she had needed years to overcome.

"I suppose I'm in the same position now," she finished, "only on the other side of the fence. I'm the other woman, you're the unfaithful husband. You know something, I honestly couldn't care less. One thing I've learned, whatever people say about you, or think about you, good or bad, kind or cruel, when you close the door at night you're on your own whether they call you the princess or the wicked witch."

Wesley listened sympathetically, relieved that she discreetly made no enquiries about the state of his own marriage.

The evening meal was fine, the bottle of wine not bad. Lorraine had come down to the bar showered, restyled, and absolutely radiant. She had let her hair down, symbolically, and changed into a tight-fitting black dress that did her no harm at all. Small wonder she had been so long upstairs, her make-up job was a dream. Wesley loved the deep red gloss lipstick and those dark eyelids that accented hair he now thought of as blond. It struck him that women have so much they can use to enhance appearance, from hair stylings and endless cosmetics for eyes, skin, mouth and nails to jewellery for ears, throat, arms, wrists, fingers, even ankles. In reply the man can shave and brush whatever hair he has left.

They went for a stroll in the grounds, both wondering why on earth someone had chosen to site a new hotel on the edge of an anonymous village like Stipsel. Apart from the coast ten miles away, and a golf course three miles distant, there seemed to be no natural attractions. The large car park with areas marked out for coaches suggested that the Abbeydene had not been built with local business in mind.

Back in their room Lorraine surprised him by producing from her case a bottle of vodka and a family size Coke. A few generous drinks later and heads were light with longing, air heavy with desire. They were within minutes, possibly seconds, of impact, abandoned carnal collision, when the sound of music, live music, a band, came up through the floor. "Oh, Wesley," she cried with delight, "they must be having a dance. Can we go down and see? Please, oh please, say Yes. I'd love a dance, just one. I haven't had a dance for years and years. I used to love dancing." She was as excited as a child.

With small candlelit tables round its perimeter and a sectional stage in place at one end, the hotel Conference Hall doubled up as a very passable ballroom. They took a table in a corner, ordered drinks from a hovering waiter, and watched half a dozen couples shuffling round to lifeless music from the deadbeat band. Next thing they were on the floor, Lorraine's arms were round his neck, and she was kissing him full on the mouth.

"I'm a bit drunk," she whispered with a little giggle, " but I think I love you, Wesley. I definitely, definitely, definitely know I want you."

Her perfume, her smooth soft arms, her warm breath in his ear. Wesley was quivering with the need of her. He closed his eyes, held her close, opened his eyes. At that moment, to the strains of *The Green Green Grass Of Home,* the nightmare began. Looking straight back at him over the rim of a large acoustic guitar was the sneery face of BRIAN POOTS, his next door neighbour, the husband of Eleanor's best friend Hilda, and the man Wesley disliked most in all the world!

Wesley had experienced shock once before. A lorry had gone out of control and was heading straight for him. He had shrunk back waiting for death, but by some miracle nothing happened. The lorry had missed him literally by inches, but Wesley had sat in his car for half an hour shaking from head to toe, his heart thumping like a steam-hammer and his head throbbing unbearably.

That was child's play compared to what he felt now at the sight of Poots. All the breath went out of him, his heart stopped, a sensation like a long slow physical sigh went right through him leaving his legs like plasticine, and a pounding spread in an instant from his neck up through the back of his head and into his temples. He was sure he was going to collapse, but Lorraine was holding him up, unaware of the terrible trauma . She may even have mistaken his shuddering for desire.

They were back in the bedroom. He had staggered to it on legs so weak and head so light that other guests must have supposed him drunk out of his mind. His hands were shaking so that he couldn't fit the card in the door and Lorraine had to open it.

"This is the night that has ruined the rest of my life," he declaimed in despair, but she seemed unable to grasp the dreadful seriousness of what was happening.

"Live dangerushly," she laughed and pawed at him hungrily.

Unbelievable, but in the midst of his anguish, his brokenness, the slag was trying to molest him. Wesley pushed her from him and she fell backwards onto the bed.

"Gently, Wesley, gently," she scolded coyly, "we've got all night." She lay back on the pillows and kicked off her shoes. "I'm all yours." She closed her eyes, and promptly fell asleep.

His mind was a torture chamber of terrible, tormenting thoughts. The big one was HOW? How could such a thing have happened? It would have been a huge, unbelievable coincidence if anyone he knew had been there at that time and place to see him with another woman, but the chances of that anyone being his next door neighbour and husband of his wife's closest friend must have been millions to one. It was the stuff of badly scripted films, poorly plotted stories. Wesley knew Poots was in some stupid band and was frequently away from home at weekends, but to think that he would be in the Abbeydene Hotel, Stipsel that evening, of all evenings.... incredible, preposterous, crazy. Was it more than coincidence? Without articulating the thought clearly in his mind Wesley found himself wondering if there was some moral force at work, some power that punished unfaithful husbands. But how could that be? He knew at least half a dozen men who had regular affairs outside marriage and got away with it as a matter of course. Was he fated to be chosen out as a loser on his very first departure from the straight and narrow?

Had he known the circumstances of the Brian Poots band being there that evening he might well have been confirmed in that belief. The advertised regular band at the Abbeydene on a Friday evening had been stricken with a flu bug, and their agent in desperation had phoned round all the bands on his books to find a replacement. The Poots band was the only one, the last resort, in truth, who could fill the vacancy. Wesley's common cold symptoms could be said to have led him to the Abbeydene, Stipsel, a flu outbreak had led to his next door neighbour being there too. Mysterious ways, and all that........

Whatever the reasons for the coincidence, the consequences were worse than human mind could bear. Wesley knew his marriage was over. They had discussed infidelity on one occasion just after they set up home, and Eleanor had made her position unequivocally clear. *One strike and you're gone. No second chances, none of the forgiving wife stuff.*

How pleased her friends would be. They had never fully accepted him, had always thought she should have done better, had settled for second best. Chances were high his job was on the line too. Eleanor's parents had used their influence and contacts to get him the position, and it was all too probable that they would reverse that process when they heard of his behaviour.

As for the Poots household, they would be delighted. Brian was a poisonous, bad-tempered little squib who disliked Wesley as heartily as Wesley despised him. Hard-faced

Hilda resented Wesley's very existence, it seemed, and would pointedly ignore him or leave the room when he entered. Had Poots phoned her already to break the good news? No, he was too tightfisted to make a long distance call, and in any case he would prefer the pleasure of telling the tale in person. A hope fluttered briefly in Wesley's frenzied brain; could something still be done to save the situation?

But what? Solution after impossible solution danced in and out, up and down, all equally impracticable: murdering Poots, suicide, full confession and plea for mercy, disappearance, bribing Poots, outright denial, lookalike/mistaken identity, twin brother, prank, acting in film, murdering Poots and Hilda, murdering Eleanor and Poots and Hilda.

Then the If Only agonies. If only he had stayed in the room, not gone down for the fatal dance. Instead of now writhing in mental torment he would be luxuriating in lustful indulgence. If only he hadn't taken that whisky, or responded to that note, or if McCrae hadn't read out that stupid advertisement...............

Accompanying these regrets was a swarm of mood swings. He wished one moment he had fulfilled his lust, so that he would have got at least something from the disaster. Next moment he was glad he had restrained himself so that he could truthfully tell Eleanor that 'nothing had happened'. The stings of shame, defiance, blame, self pity, guilt, rage, sorrow, hate and fear, all battled to inflame further the wound of his burning mind.

Wesley never went without his Paracetamol and he washed down four of them now with the remaining Coke. He was so jittery that the bottle rattled against his teeth. He knew the tablets would do nothing to ease the excruciating pain in his head that felt like an axe was buried in the back of his skull. The nerves in his stomach tumbled and turned like a washing machine.

His thoughts turned to the fat woman on the bed who had destroyed his life, his future. She was snoring, her garish red mouth slack with sleep below the straw hair. Her thick make-up, like a clown's, had smeared the pillow. Grotesque, disgusting. What was it she had said, that she honestly didn't care what people said or thought about her? So that was it, her life was a wreck and now she had wrecked his too. How had he been so foolish to risk everything for a woman like that? A wave of nausea swept through him.

It was about half three. In desperation to combat his relentless mental and nervous suffering Wesley had finished the bottle of vodka neat and he could now add to his tally of afflictions an acidic burning in throat and chest. He felt he was going to be sick, but was afraid of waking the woman still snoring steadily on the bed.

There was a Gents at the other end of the corridor. He could make it down there. The hotel was quiet, and the corridor dimly lit. Wesley reached the toilet on unsteady legs, but couldn't be sick, not even by sticking his fingers down his throat. He had a pee to justify the journey and was just started back towards his room when a bedroom door opened quietly and a woman slipped out in practised fashion. The door closed quickly behind her, but not before Wesley had glimpsed inside the hated countenance of his nemesis, BRIAN POOTS. What's more, Poots had seen him and a flicker of fear crossed his face just as the door closed over.

Wesley's heart thumped so loudly he felt it was going to explode. He controlled his whirling head and gently knocked the door. There was a pause. Wesley was just about to knock again when it opened and Poots was there before him. They faced each other without a word. Then two enemies solemnly shook hands to seal a vow of mutual silence in the interests of the common good.

Two hundred miles away and at about the same time as Wesley made it back to his hotel room, Eleanor kissed her lover goodnight. It was the work of minutes to slip out of Hilda's bed, through the side exit and gap in the fence, and into the security of her own bed next door.

THE SEAGULL

Sara replaced the phone with a little giggle of excitement. An invitation to 'come round for a quick coffee' from Janet meant only one thing, news, and news from Janet meant only one thing, a new man in her life. Sara pictured her friend at the other end of the line, twisting her hair into some startling shape or practising a seductive pout as she prepared to set sail once more in her endless quest for Mr Right.

Odd, Sara thought, but even the most happily married new wives, and she counted herself firmly in that category, still missed, in some odd way, the thrill, the uncertainty, of the chase. There was Janet, desperate for a steady and committed relationship, and here she was, vicariously enjoying the vagaries and vicissitudes of her friend's frantic dating programme. Sara felt almost a little guilty for having the best of both worlds, as if she were selfishly enjoying Janet from the sidelines, but then reminded herself that she was providing a valuable listening and advisory service for her friend. One thing was certain, if this new relationship were to be like all its predecessors, it was going to be complicated and short-lived.

Sara allowed herself another little guilty giggle. The simple truth was, Janet was fun. She never tried to be, but in Sara's eyes she was consistently and irresistibly funny, especially in her romantic adventures.

The omens were good. Janet had met Jonathan at the library's Book Club, one of the few remaining mixed local societies that she had not previously exhausted. Its members were invited to read one of several suggested novels and report back on it at the next meeting to the rest of the group.

Janet was bubbly. "Wasn't it a coincidence we both chose to read the same one? And our opinions were so similar. I was worried when I heard 'Jonathan', it was too like John. Janet and John. Can you imagine that? *Janet and John Go To the Library*. But then when I thought about it, it was OK. Janet and Jonathan. Almost like we were designed to go together. What d'you think?"

There it was again, an impulse in Sara to laugh at the wrong moment, but Janet had gained a froth moustache from her cappuccino and this, in tandem with the pure riot of her new frizzy hair style, was so much at odds with the serious dark eyes and earnest delivery that Sara had to camouflage her smile in a cough.

"Anyhow, we chatted after the meeting and he seemed nice, and we arranged to meet on Wednesday after lunch. There's another good sign. We both have half days on Wednesdays. I've a real good feeling about this one. What d'you think?"

Sara knew no opinion was wanted or needed. She of course could have pointed out that Janet had had a good feeling about the previous dozen or so dates, but instead she wished her friend every success and was given in return a promise of a full post-match report.

Sara was going spare late Wednesday afternoon over the problems presented by a faulty washing machine so that when the phone rang and she heard Janet's 'Don't even ask me' she was momentarily at a loss.

"Can you come over, Sara? I need to talk to somebody sensible after the antics I've just been through. Drop everything and come on over. You'll be back home in good time to make Ray his tea."

Janet looked funnier than ever, the perfect make-up, false eyelashes and lacquered hair contrasting with the homely little apron which she had considered necessary for the making of a pot of coffee. Sara settled into her usual seat and her usual role as audience.

"I know you don't like cigarettes, Sara, but I don't care, I need one now to calm me down." Janet took a deep drag and sighed out a cloud of smoke.

"So how did it go?" Sara prompted.

"Fine, for the first ten minutes. He was waiting for me outside Morrison's and I thought he looked nice, casual, polo shirt, light coloured jacket and chinos to match. I gave him the benefit of the doubt over the sandals, they went OK with the rest of the outfit.

It's as well I had these on my feet, because he suggested a walk along the beach. I liked the way he walked me on the inside along the promenade. He didn't take my hand, or put his arm round me or anything like that, but I figured he was either too shy or too polite on our first date."

Janet took another puff of her cigarette and washed it down with a mouthful of coffee.

"We were walking and talking quite nicely, thank you, finding out about each other's jobs, interests, brothers and sisters, all the usual early stuff. I felt good, and smelt good, was looking good and starting to think Jonathan was maybe a bit of all right, when everything went to pieces.

Can you believe, I was the one who started the whole thing off. Out of the corner of my eye I noticed something white flapping about up among the rocks just ahead of us. Jonathan hadn't seen it and, I'll never know why, I drew his attention to it. We both clambered over the rocks and seaweed and there it was, one of those big seagull things, fluttering and scrabbling about and trying to get away from us. One of its wings was dragging behind it and its leg seemed broken, so that it couldn't move straight but went sort of sideways, like a crab or something.

I wanted to go on and leave it there, but Jonathan felt sorry for it and tried to lift it. You should have seen him scrambling after it, and when he tried to pick it up it made these squawking noises and tried to peck him with its big red and yellow beak. I didn't realise before how big seagulls are.

Anyway, he managed to lift it, and it kept twisting its head round and glaring up at him and trying to get at him with that beak. It looked really vicious and ungrateful. Its dirty feet and wings were making a right mess of his clothes, and I told him to put it down and leave it, but he said he wanted to help it. Can you imagine? And that was only the start of it."

Janet took a last draw of her cigarette and dropped the remains in her coffee.

"So, what did he do?"

"He set the thing down again and messed about on his mobile for about ten minutes until he got through to some wild life place or bird sanctuary or something. All the time he was on the phone the seagull was getting away from us, and we had to keep following. Jonathan looked really silly scrabbling over the rocks in his sandals, one arm holding the phone to his ear, the other out balancing like a tightrope walker. They told him they could do nothing for the injured seagull and the kindest thing he could do was kill it. He was whiter than the seagull when he passed on that piece of information, I can tell you. He wasn't expecting to hear that he was going to have to kill it.

'How am I supposed to kill it? I've never killed anything in my life. I don't know anything about killing things.' And so he went on and on, more or less asking me what to do. I remembered my old grandmother killing turkeys at Christmas, wringing their necks, and told him how she used to do it, so he managed to catch the seagull again and tried pulling and twisting its neck, but, every time he stopped, it untwisted its neck, looked up really aggressively, and took another peck at him. The whole thing was laughable.

We were right next to one of the rockpools, you remember the ones we used to paddle in when we were kids? Well, I suggested he drown the thing in it, and he looked relieved that he wouldn't have to go back to the neck wringing bit. Need I tell you what happened? No matter how long he held that bird's head under the water, when he let it go and it came back up again, feathers all straggly and limp, it would suddenly start shaking itself and squawking again and trying to break free. It was amazing. In all honesty, you couldn't have blamed Jonathan this time, the thing seemed 'undrownable'.

The two of us just stood there among the rocks looking at each other, with the gull still shrieking and trying to escape. It was ridiculous.

'Get a stone and kill it,' I told him. He hesitated, but then started looking for a stone to do the job. Can you believe it, we couldn't find a suitable stone on that whole beach. There were millions of pebbles, small and round and smooth, but not one decent sized rock. Jonathan tried hitting the seagull on the head a few times with one of the pebbles, but his blows were feeble and only seemed to make the thing angrier. By this stage, if we had found a rock, I think I might have hit him with it instead of the bird.

Needless to say, it was left to me to find the answer. We buried it! We scooped a big hole in the sand, dumped the seagull in it, and scraped the loose sand back in on top of it. The whole time the seagull was trying to flap its way out, and screeching at us, but we finally got it covered over and the sand levelled. Can you picture it, me in my best top and gypsy skirt down on my knees on the beach ladling handfuls of wet sand over a scraggly, crippled seagull, my lovely nails job a wreck, all broken and full of sand. It was a nightmare, Sara, a nightmare.

We sat there for a few minutes in silence. He was breathing so hard I thought maybe he was sobbing or something. We tried to go on with the walk, but the whole thing was ruined. The squawks of the seagull were still ringing in my head, and my clothes were in a right state. Jonathan mooched along without saying anything. The date was a disaster. I suppose you know what's coming now?"

"Not really," said Sara, and meant it.

"I should have guessed it, of course. Looking back, all the signs were there. Yes. I should have seen it coming. Out of the blue, Jonathan suddenly stops, looks over at me, and tells me, wait for it, tells me he's gay."

"What? Gay? Why did he go out with you if he's gay?"

"Good question. When I got my breath back, I asked him that. You know what he said? He wanted to talk more about the books he likes and what novels I enjoy. As if I give a toss about his bloody books. I turned on my heel and left him there. A pity I couldn't have buried him in that hole along with the seagull. Should I have slapped his face before I walked off? What d'you think?"

But Sara wasn't thinking much about anything, not the poor buried bird or the soft-hearted gay young man; all she knew was that something was changed, lost for ever, that she would never be able to find her funny friend Janet funny again.

MAGGIE

Just one more to go, No 38, and then goodbye, and good riddance, to Trinidad Street. Sam gave an ironic laugh. Trinidad Street. How on earth did they come up with that name for this sunless, tottering twin row of jerry-built backstreet houses? What twisted sense of humour had been at work when these slums had been thrown up and graced with that exotic nameplate?

It was as though fancy titles could somehow disguise the drab anonymity and squalor in working-class warrens of sub-standard housing. Already that week Sam had cleared for demolition such improbably named streets as Vicarage Row, Geneva Street and, wait for it, Palace Gardens!

He checked his file. No 38, single occupant. He hoped the Social Worker would be there early to get the thing wrapped up quickly.

How times had changed since he had joined the company as a young man over thirty years ago. In those days a red pen went through whole areas, eviction orders went out, the bulldozers went in, and redevelopment was under way in a matter of months, sometimes weeks. Now there was an army out there of organised do-gooders, all designed to throw a spanner in the works: Citizens' Advice, Tenants' Rights, Housing Groups, Residents' Committees and more public bodies than you could throw a trowel at. Next thing they'd be providing not just a Social Worker, but solicitor, lawyer, the works.

He glanced at the paper work. Mrs Agnes Fullerton, widow, aged 73. It looked good. She had only lived there for a couple of years, so there should be none of that daft sentimentality that prompted people to resist being rehoused. If all went well he could be cleared up about two, and treat himself to a good pub lunch in The Galleon.

Sam recognised the Datsun parked outside 38. His luck was in. Florence was the only Social Worker worth a damn. The rest were wishy-washy women who hid behind bureaucratic box-ticking, and wimpy young men, university refugees mostly, who were all too ready to retreat to the safety of the office at the first hint of aggression or threat to their person. Florence answered his knock and nodded him in.

Over the years Sam had been in hundreds, possibly thousands, of houses identical to this one, but he never failed to wonder every time how whole generations of large families had managed to live and love and fight and breed in these dark, pokey boxes that they called home. There they were, the 'good' front room, or 'parlour', the living room at the back with lean-to scullery attached, and the narrow stairs leading up to two cramped bedrooms. For the life of him Sam could never comprehend why anyone would prefer these cold, basic conditions to the new modern homes they were entitled to by law.

He had no problems with Agnes Fullerton, a tidy, nervous little woman who seemed sensible, compliant and keen to get out of 38 Trinidad Street. Sam and Florence did the business quickly in the front room, declined the cup of tea she offered, and were getting ready to leave when she stopped them in their tracks.

"What's going to happen to Maggie?"

"Maggie," said Sam, "who's Maggie?"

"She lives here. Does she have to go with me?" The question implied that this was not something Mrs Fullerton wanted.

Sam raised an eyebrow to Florence who shrugged and shook her head.

"Where's Maggie now?" Sam asked.

"She's here. Will she go with me?"

Florence caught Sam's eye and pointed discreetly to the little cuckoo clock on the wall. Sam got the message.

"Now don't you worry about Maggie, Mrs Fullerton. We'll take care of her. You just worry about yourself."

"But what's going to happen to her? Where is she going to go?"

Sam winked over to Florence. He would handle this. "Maggie? No problem. I'll take her home with me. She can move in with me."

The woman was trembling. "Thank you, son, thank you. But you'll have to ask her. You have to invite her to go and live with you. She won't go if you don't ask her."

Sam theatrically pronounced the invitation, hamming it up for comic effect. "Maggie, will you come with me and live under my humble roof. You will be welcome in the home of Sam Collier."

Florence was trying to disguise her laughter as a cough when little Mrs Fullerton inexplicably burst into uncontrollable sobbing.

It wasn't often Sam left a 'client' with such a good feeling. As often as not words such as 'heartless bastard' would be ringing in his ears. This annoyed him, but only a tiny bit. He couldn't have cared less what they called him or thought of him, but it was the frustration of failing to make them see simple common sense that got to him. There he was trying to improve their lives and lot in a real, practical way, offering warm, comfortable and secure accommodation, and they in return responded either with open defiance and hostility, or with grudging acceptance as though they were doing him the favour. Sam took his job seriously, and genuinely believed that he was advancing social progress and the march of civilisation.....

As sure as there's an eye in a goat, he had caught a bug or chill or something in that little rabbit hutch of a house. Sam wasn't one to pay attention to coughs or sneezes, but to be so skin cold on such a clammy, sticky day told him something was amiss. A couple of large hot whiskeys when he got home would sort it. He shivered and checked the car heater in case it was blowing cold air, but nothing was wrong there.

Something else was wrong with the car, however, the bloody radio. Sam had turned it on in the hope of catching a bit of cricket commentary, but had got instead about ten seconds of Dusty Springfield before a terrible static hissing and crackling started. He changed stations and found the cricket, clear as a bell. Back to Dusty, and back to the same infuriating interference. Must be a fault with the broadcast or the reception. Over to another station, some woman reading a story for infants, and the same static racket. Sam swore with feeling. Intermittent fault, the worst kind to get fixed. He'd leave it in to some smart-ass mechanic, and it would be working perfectly. Total nuisance.

By the end of the day Sam would happily have settled for just a faulty car radio. He had gone straight home, his hunger having left him, and put the kettle on. He was out of cloves. Sam liked cloves in his hot whiskey. He nipped out to the corner store and got a few other items as well. Funny, but as he stood at the check-out the chill had left him, the shivering had stopped. It was when he got back to the flat that the sequence started. As soon as he opened the door, it hit him, an icy coldness that almost took his breath away. How was this happening? There had to be something wrong with him, because the flat was the warmest, cosiest place on earth. Like the radio, he must have an intermittent fault. Sam managed a grim smile.

The hot whiskey was good, really good, but did nothing to counter the cold. The odd thing was that Sam didn't feel any inner symptoms; it was more like the kind of surface chill felt on a winter day, an icy fog on the skin. He fixed himself another hot whiskey and occupied his favourite armchair. An insidious weariness settled on him. It wasn't a pleasant weariness, more like the strength was going out of him.

Eartha Kitt. Just the ticket. For such a hard-headed man's man, Sam had very frilly, feminine tastes in music. He slid the *Bad but Beautiful* CD in, closed his eyes, and waited for the familiar silky tones to soothe away the day's frustrations. Eartha was just starting on the title track when she was almost drowned out completely by the same loud static disturbance that had overwhelmed the car radio's output. Now it was amplified through Sam's elaborate seven speaker set-up.

What the hell was happening? It was unbelievable. The system was working beautifully the previous evening. Sam ejected the disc and tried it again. Worse, if anything. He skipped through all the tracks. No improvement.

Wait a bit, what about the TV? Surely it couldn't be faulty too? No, thank heavens, there was the afternoon horse racing from Haydock, the commentator's laundered tones smooth and clear. Sam idly flicked to another channel and instantly wished he hadn't. The same riot of sound interference seemed to mock Delia's efforts as she laid bare the mysteries of successful puff pastry.

Sam's frustration and helplessness found relief in rage. He switched the TV off, threw the hand-set into the corner, swore savagely, and threatened revenge on all those suppliers who had sold him such a heap of top of the range, state of the art rubbish.

He turned the heating on. At least something was working properly. The room gradually warmed enough for him to feel a little better. But why should he need burning hot radiators on such a muggy day?

He remembered that Angela was coming round in the evening. He'd better put her off until he felt his normal healthy self; wouldn't want her to catch whatever it was he had.

He rang her work number.

"Hello, yours truly. You'll never guess, but I'm not well. Don't laugh. Some kind of chill or flu or something."

She did laugh. "Glad to hear you're human after all. Look, I've a nice casserole ready, and I'm not going to eat it by myself. I'll come round tomorrow evening, unless I hear you're still under the weather. My money's on you being right as rain in the morning."

"Great. Sounds good. Sorry about this, Angela, but….." He got no further. An audio blizzard wiped him out. The phone too was on the blink! He couldn't believe it. What next?

In truth, Sam could have coped all right with the aggro and inconvenience of equipment failure. Much of his work was confrontational in nature, and he could handle himself well in disputation over faulty goods, even derive some satisfaction from getting things sorted out. What he couldn't deal with was there being something wrong with himself. Like most strong men who despise sickness or any kind of indisposition, Sam was unprepared and unsuited to deal with it when it came. Illness, however slight, made him feel weak, vulnerable.

The feeling that he had some kind of infection or fever deepened as the evening wore on. He kept getting the impression that there was somebody else in the room with him. It was more than a fancy, it was ALMOST a sighting. He could nearly see someone or something right on the edge of his vision, but when he looked quickly round there was nothing there. Yet the notion was so strong that Sam started to think he was definitely hallucinating. The odd thing was that he had no sickness, no high temperature or headache, none of the usual accompaniments.

He found himself reaching down Karen's photograph from the wall. Sam may never have realised it or admitted it, but even on her deathbed she had been the strong one, stronger than the big man holding her hand and giving assurances that neither of them believed.

Something was wrong with his vision! Whatever it was that was afflicting him, it was affecting his eyesight. He was holding the framed picture of the woman he had loved and married, but no matter how hard he tried, or at what distance he held the photo, he could not see it clearly. The image was blurred, indistinct. Everything else in the room was clearly defined, but the picture just would not focus. When he turned it over the cardboard backing was pin sharp, but as soon as he reversed it his wife's face swam instantly into muzziness.

Sam's head reeled with the effort of finding focus. A kind of fear was growing in him. He hung the photograph back up and went to bed.

If he was hoping for a good night's sleep to put the stresses of the day behind him, he was badly mistaken. As soon as his head hit the pillow his ear was invaded by an insistent kind of whispering sound that he could ALMOST identify as words. Yet, try as he might, that last tiny connection that would make everything clear eluded him. It was a bit like not being able to remember someone's name, to be oh so close, to have it right on the tip of the memory's tongue, inches from the Finish and not able to cross the line. Sam lay wide awake.

Some of the songs he loved best had lyrics that he could not make out, no matter how often he listened to them. He had to invent his own words to fill the gaps. This was similar. Hour after hour he heard the whispering sounds, over and over, but he could not pin them down. He lay in a state of nervous exhaustion. He was never sure afterwards if he got any sleep that night or not.

Angela had said he'd probably be 'as right as rain' next day. How wrong could she be! Barring the day he had laid Karen to rest, it turned out to be the worst day of his fifty two years. What linked the two days for him was the same kind of heaviness of heart. After the loss of Karen he had chosen to ignore the opinions of friends who diagnosed his blackness of mood as depression. Nonsense. Depression was something for wasters who wanted time off work. What he was feeling was sadness, pure old-fashioned sadness.

"I've had my heart broken," Sam said. "It'll need its own time to mend".

This was another matter altogether, however. Irritation at faulty equipment came nowhere near accounting for the dispiritedness that seemed to sap the will from him.

He made a couple of calls, noting that the phone was fine, and then decided he'd take the day off. His caseload was up to date and he hadn't missed a day through sickness in years. He called the office.

"Liz, I'll not…." was as far as he got. The bloody phone was away again, spitting and crackling like a bonfire. He couldn't hear Liz above it, and she undoubtedly couldn't hear him. Rage. Bafflement.

The laughable thing was that he rang the phone company to report that the phone wasn't working! He did it automatically, like trying to switch the light on to find the candles during a power cut. They promised to send somebody out, and thankfully didn't ask where he was calling from.

He tried the CD Player again, opting this time for Nana Mouskouri. Worse than ever, he could hardly hear her voice at all above the static. To compound his misery, that dreadful unintelligible whispering sound in his ear, which seemed to have disappeared, returned with a vengeance. Now it was more a sensation than a sound, like someone stage whispering too closely into his ear.

As he had feared, when the telephone engineer arrived about eleven the damned thing was working perfectly. The man was thorough and tried all the tests in his repertoire, but couldn't find even a suspicion of a fault. The only benefit Sam got from the visit had nothing to do with the phone. The engineer had arrived in shirt sleeves but half way though his routine had gone out to his van and come back wearing a company jacket. He made no comment, which prompted Sam to ask the question.

"Do you find it cold in here?"

The man hesitated, looked around, and settled for the simple truth. "Freezing. There's something wrong with your ventilation, or air conditioning, or heating, or something, I don't know, but it's like an oven outside and like an icebox in here."

So the cold was in the air, the atmosphere, not in him. But how, why? After all, he had felt it first in the car, not in the flat. In any case, the flat was so well insulated that normally the challenge lay in keeping it cool.

Next man in was the sound system technician, a perky brat with a ring through his eyebrow. He only half listened to Sam's recital of the machine's eccentricities, produced a test disc, slotted it in, twiddled with the controls, and hey presto, performance perfect. A smirk appeared which Sam perversely hoped Eartha or Nana would wipe off, but instead they never sounded better. Sam volunteered a Peggy Lee as the test clincher, and she was exquisite. No glitch of any sort.

" Do people actually listen to this stuff?" asked the brat, leafing through Sam's CD collection. It was clearly a rhetorical question. "It's as well you're still under guarantee, mate, or I'd be hittin' you for a forty smackers call-out fee," he added.

"Do you think it's cold in here?" from Sam.

"Cold? I wouldn't say it's cold. I'd probably say it's Baltic. Even my goose bumps have goose bumps."

Sam appreciated the old joke, not for its wit but for its import. There was no doubt about it, the fault wasn't in him. For some mysterious reason his flat had suddenly turned Arctic. Bad news can sometimes be welcome.

Sam's improvement in mood lasted for only a matter of minutes. When the brat had left he sat down to listen to some of the 'stuff' and he was right back to square one. The noise was back and worse than before, if that were possible. The only comfort was that the din was actually better than the whispering effect in his ear. Or was it head? Or mind? Or, worst of all, imagination? For the first time Sam started to question his own mental state.

He had to wait until late in the afternoon before the television engineer arrived. Sam had tried different programmes several times and there was definitely an intermittent fault affecting both sound and picture. One minute the quality of both was top class, next thing the sound was pandemonium and the picture was nothing but fuzz. Against all common sense Sam hoped the set would misbehave now the engineer was here.

It didn't. The image and sound quality on every channel was impeccable.

"Can't find anything wrong here, boss," said the fat engineer. "Are you sure you had the aerial in?"

The flat being so cold, and himself feeling so miserable, Sam should have further postponed Angela's visit, but, selfishly, he allowed her to come round that evening. He really did need someone to talk to, and nobody was more fit for that purpose than Angela. Sam and she were the classic 'just good friends', each happy to have the companionship of the other with no strings attached.

Angela had been Karen's best friend since girlhood, even though they had gone to different schools and pursued different careers. Angela's husband had run off with his secretary, which served to fortify their friendship even further.

As soon as she stepped in through the door Angela stopped dead and looked at Sam with alarm on her face.

"Sam, what's wrong?"

"Well, I've got a kind of buzzing thing in my ears and I'm feeling a bit down, but….."

"No, I don't mean that," she interrupted. "What's happened? There's something wrong. Something's not right in this room. I can feel it."

"I know. It's the heating, or the lack of it. The temperature's away down in here, has been for a day or so. Can't explain it."

Sam ushered her into the kitchen. The whispering in his head was getting worse. He felt odd, nervy. The weariness and dejection of the previous evening came again upon him. He poured two glasses of wine, but Angela looked distinctly ill at ease, and took her drink from him mechanically. Sam tried some conversation, but she wasn't listening. She handed him the large carrier bag she had brought.

"I'm sorry, Sam. I can't stay. I have to get out of here, I have to go."

"What? You've only just arrived. What about our meal?"

Sam had never seen her so upset, and so quickly too. He couldn't understand it, and tried to persuade her to stay, but she was almost desperate to leave.

"Heat the casserole for yourself, and call me tomorrow, Sam. I'm sorry." Then she was past him and through the door and gone.

The rest of the evening went rapidly downhill. Sam finished the bottle of wine for comfort, and heated the casserole dish in the microwave. He set the table and miserably served the meal for himself, the whispering in his head louder than ever and, he fancied, angry in tone. At that point, on top of everything else, he found he had lost his sense of taste! Angela was a wonderful cook, in all honesty better than Karen had ever been, but her delicious looking coq au vin was totally tasteless.

A kind of mild panic spread through Sam. What was wrong with him? Buzzing in his ears, selective absence of focus in his eyesight, lowness of spirit, anxiety, and now loss of taste. How had everything gone out of kilter all at once? He had never known anything like it.

He tried to phone Angela. She answered immediately, but after a few words their attempted conversation was completely swamped by the now familiar crackle and hiss. Sam was close to despair in his frustration.

He definitely got no sleep at all that night. He had once read somewhere the theory that the worst fear a man can have is the fear of going mad, of losing mental control and not being able to stop it happening. Sam's hours of troubled tossing and turning supported the theory.

It was a measure of his concern that early next morning he rang his doctor, something he couldn't remember having ever done before. The phone line was as clear as crystal. By good fortune there had been a cancellation, and Sam got an appointment for ten o'clock that morning.

Dr Britten was sensible and experienced. He was looking at Sam's file, and nodded to him to sit down.

"It's as well I haven't too many patients like you, Mr Collier. I'd be out of business in less than a week. Must be something special has brought you in?"

Sam already felt a bit of a sham. His gloom had lifted appreciably and the whispering was gone from his ears. To justify his visit, however, he recounted everything, even including his impression of there being someone else in the room. He made no mention of the problems he was experiencing with the various items of equipment. It would have sounded childish.

To his credit, Britten heard him through, giving little almost imperceptible nods now and then. When Sam had ended, the doctor asked him to lie on the couch.

"You're ready for your M.O.T.," he said, and set about it with professional enthusiasm, taking heart soundings and blood pressure, testing respiration, looking in ears, eyes, mouth, tapping and listening, and finishing up weighing him on the floor scales. "Now, the nurse will give you a blood test on your way out, otherwise your long-overdue overhaul is complete."

"What's the verdict, doctor?" asked Sam, buttoning up his shirt.

"In a minute. First, tell me about your job, the hours you work, your time off, conditions, and anything else there is to tell."

Again Britten listened closely until he judged Sam had finished.

"A few years ago the buzz word in this business was *virus*," he said. "Everybody had a virus of one kind or another. Today it's *stress*. Everybody has time off with stress, is stressed out, is suffering from stress. If we doctors aren't sure, all we need to do is to diagnose stress and everybody's happy.

The difference with you, Mr Collier, is that you are a classic stress case. I could use you as a teaching aid on the signs and symptoms of stress. I can sit here now and tell you with full confidence that it's stress you're suffering from. Physically you're as sound as a drum. It's nervous exhaustion and a build up of mental fatigue that have you the way you've described to me.

I could send you away from here now with a prescription for any number of pills and medicines, but I'm not going to. What I am going to prescribe is at least two weeks' complete rest, away from work and ideally on a relaxing holiday somewhere. A bus tour, something like that. You need a break from the pressure of your job."

Part of Sam wanted to retort that he loved his job and would be up-tight away from it, but he was so relieved to learn that there was nothing seriously the matter with him that he readily accepted the doctor's analysis and recommendation. After his blood test he actually left the surgery with a spring in his step. Dr Britten had been so sure in his assessment that it never occurred to Sam for a moment to doubt it.

Sam called round to his workplace and made a few arrangements with Liz at the desk. He called Angela from his office.

"Sam! Thank God. I've been so worried about you. I've been calling you all morning. I have to see you. It's really important."

"Don't worry about me. I've been to the doc. Clean bill of health. Well, almost."

"No, Sam, it's not that. Where are you? Can we meet? Like now?"

Sam bought two large coffees to go, and met her in the park as arranged. She was in a sombre mood, in contrast with the brightly coloured borders glowing in the sun.

"Sam, you have to listen to me. Please listen. I felt so guilty leaving you on your own last night with whatever it is."

"What?"

"Sam, you must listen to this. There's something or somebody evil in your flat. I'm sure of it. I sensed it the minute I arrived. It's very strong, and it resented me being there. No, more than that, it hated me. Sam, you have to believe me. You know I wouldn't lie to you."

Sam was confused. He had never heard her speak like this before.

"Sam, there's a side to me I've never spoken about to you, because it's not the kind of thing you'd have any time for or interest in. You see, I've always been sensitive to ….things. I mean, influences, atmospheres, the aura or ambience of people and places, that kind of thing.

You think I'm talking nonsense. Let me give you an example. When I was at Convent School there was a girl who didn't like me. She never said or did anything to show it, but I felt her dislike like you would feel a cool breeze on a warm day. I think she was jealous of me, for some reason known only to herself. One day when I came into the classroom I felt hatred in it, thick and real and cold. Nobody said a word, but I could feel it in the air, on my skin, in my nose and mouth. It was like a sixth sense, as I've heard it called. I found out later she had told the class a vile lie about me and poisoned them against me.

Sam, that was the feeling I got yesterday the minute I stepped into your flat, only a hundred times stronger, a hundred times more vicious and venomous. I lost my faith years ago, as you know, but there's still enough of the good Catholic girl left to tell me when I'm faced by a force that means me harm. Sam, there was a definite presence in your flat. You can see why I'm worried for you."

Sam was silent, at a loss to know what to say or do. As a staunch non-believer, a total what-you-see-is-all-there-is person, he found it difficult to respond to Angela's alarm. He suddenly wanted to get away from her.

"Sam, please don't go back home until you've thought about this. What about the cold in the flat? How d'you explain that? There must be other things you've noticed. Please come round to mine, even for the rest of the day. Whatever it is might go away if there's nobody there."

Sam looked around. Young mothers were pushing small children on the play swings, a pigeon was pecking up crumbs near his feet, traffic was roaring like the sea in the distance. The things Angela was talking about were unreal, irrelevant, impossible. He finished his coffee.

"Thanks for meeting me, Angela. And for the casserole last night. It was delicious. And for your concern for me. But look, I have to get back to work, I've catching up to do. I'll ring you later."

He stood up, kissed her on the cheek, and walked away. As he did so he thought he heard her offering him the name of a priest.

Sam ignored doctor's orders and did the half dozen preliminary calls he had arranged with Liz. Contrary to what the doc had said, it was refreshing being back in the swing of things. Like most people, Sam sometimes complained about routine, but complained more seriously when something happened to interrupt it. He was feeling almost back to normal, and the icing on the cake was finding that the car radio and CD were working perfectly.

Yet the meeting with Angela troubled him. Her earnestness had reached him more than he had admitted to himself, and that psychic part of her was new and strange to him. Could there be something in what she had said? What was causing the coldness in the flat, and why were the items of equipment misbehaving? But wait a bit. Imagine Sam Collier going into work and telling his colleagues that his flat was haunted, possessed; he'd be the laughing stock of the whole building. Sam shook his head and drove home.

Was he getting used to it, or was the coldness in the flat not just so bad? He knew a very good heating and home insulation man, and would get him to call some time over the weekend.

Apart from the odd sense again that right in the corner of his vision was some shape or figure which wasn't there when he looked, Sam felt fairly well. Although the mental weariness and despondency were gone he was physically tired, and went to bed early after a light meal.

Sam woke in a cold sweat. There was someone in the bed beside him. He knew it just as he knew the wardrobe was standing in the corner. The only difference was he could see the wardrobe. The surprising thing was how small that difference was, how little it meant.

The bedside clock's green figures showed 2.22. Sam didn't know what had woken him so abruptly. It was like someone or something had nudged him without touching him. His heart was thumping so strongly he wondered that he couldn't hear it in the stillness of the room.

His absolute conviction that there was someone lying beside him meant only one thing: Angela was right. There was a 'presence', as she had called it. He lay in the half light and went over in his mind the things she had said.

Wait a minute, she had mentioned jealousy in her story. Did that suggest the thing or person in his flat was a woman? Suddenly it struck him. That screwy old woman in Trinidad Street. Of course, why had he not thought of it sooner? Probably because he was meeting all kinds of eccentrics and nutters in the course of his everyday work. How could he have connected the ramblings of some old dear with the aberrations of his heating system or electronic equipment? But, no doubt about it, everything had definitely started after he had invited her 'friend' to come home with him! What was her name? Peggy. No. Think, think, think. Maggie. That was it, Maggie.

An idea came to him. He slid out of bed and went through to the lounge. He inserted a Perry Como disc into the audio system. Perfect, flawless reproduction. So too with Al Martino. Taking a deep breath he slid in a Nina Simone. Almost instantly *Feeling Good* was drowned by the cacophony he both feared and half-hoped to hear. He ejected the CD and waited for the whispering to start in his head. It did. She was scolding him! Already he was thinking in terms of 'she'.

Funny how she had waited until after the disc had stopped before scolding him. It was as if she had been putting all her powers into destroying the song, and had to wait to 're-charge' before turning them on him.

Sam waited a few moments and then closed his eyes and said aloud in a penitent voice, "I'm sorry, Maggie. I won't do it again."

For a minute or so nothing happened. Sam felt a bit foolish and was wondering if he should repeat the apology when he heard or felt the whispering start to recede, like anger slowly subsiding. Sam sat on his knees, in his pyjamas, in front of the console, like a guilty schoolboy suitably reprimanded for his naughtiness.

It was after half past two in the morning but he rang Angela. He could tell by her instant answer and alertness that she hadn't been sleeping, was wide awake.

"Sam? What's wrong? Are you OK?" There was panic in her voice.

"William, you remember that problem we were talking about in the park earlier? I think you were right. I'm going to consult an expert today to see if I can find a solution."

"Sam, are you all right? Who's William? What's going on?"

"It's OK, William. I'll call you later."

"Come in, Mr Collier. I've been expecting you." Mrs Fullerton led him into the parlour of her Trinidad Street home. In a matter of weeks it would be a pile of rubble.

"You know why I've come back to see you, Agnes?"

"Yes, of course. I knew you'd come back to find out about Maggie. I'm sorry, son, but I couldn't resist when you offered to take her home. It was your idea. You suggested it. You didn't know you were offering me a way out of my torment."

For a frail, elderly woman supposedly a bit barmy Mrs Fullerton sounded remarkably composed compared to her manner on Sam's previous visit. There was a certain well-bred quality in her demeanour and speech that had escaped him earlier, perhaps because he always assumed that people living in such houses were necessarily low class and uneducated.

"Tell me about Maggie, everything you know."

"Which isn't much. Everything I know I've had to learn for myself, the hard way. I know nothing at all about who she is, or was, or how she came to be the way she is now."

Sam was disappointed. He knew by experience that she was telling the truth.

"What have you learned, then? I need to know."

"How to cope, what to do and not to do. How to live with her, her strengths and her weaknesses. I'll tell you her weaknesses first, if you like. She doesn't know what you're thinking. She can see what you do, and hear what you say, but she doesn't know what you're thinking. Another thing, she can't hurt you. That's not how she works. She can't touch or move or change things. Except the coldness. She can't hide that, it's part of her. It's her giveaway. She's crafty, but she can't hide that."

"Crafty?"

"Yes, when she has to be. She'll hide what she can do from other people. She didn't like me listening to the wireless and she would ruin the broadcasts. I told my neighbours about it, but when they came in she allowed the programmes to go ahead the very best. People started to think I was a bit mental."

Sam nodded. He recognised the tactic all too clearly.

"Jealousy, you see. She wanted me all to herself. She lost me all my friends. I used to stay out all day long, going to the pictures or walking round the big Shopping Centres, but when I came back she would punish me. Sometimes she was so hard I thought I was going out of my mind altogether."

"Punish you. How did she do that?"

"The whispering. Has she not started the whispering yet? Over and over in your ear and brain until you beg her to stop. You can't make out what she says, but it's not good, you can be sure of that."

"Why did you not leave her, move house, leave her behind?"

Mrs Fullerton gave a sad little smile. "It's not as easy as that. I tried it, but only once. You see, I've only been here in this house for about two years. I used to live in another town up north. That's where I met her. I moved here to try to get away from her. For a week I was free of her. Then one night the whispering started again, cruel, terrible. She had found me, don't ask me how. I had to promise never to go away again in order to get the whispering to stop. She's like an infection, or a disease, that catches up with you no matter where you go."

Sam was glued to every word. "You say you met Maggie up north. How?"

"I was tricked into it. After my husband died I was short of money and, as they say, I came down in the world. I discovered he had debts I knew nothing about, and I had to sell the bungalow to pay them off. The estate agent told me about a terrace house going cheap and I went to see it. Apart from being a bit cold, it was all right, and I agreed to buy it. The owner told me he had a cat called Maggie that he didn't want to take with him, and he asked me if I would like it for company. I said OK, and he said all I had to do was to say, 'Maggie, you're going to live with me now. You're mine now,' and she would appear. You know of course what I got instead. That's how I knew to tell you that you had to invite Maggie home with you."

"Did you ever get in touch with the man who tricked you?"

"I tried. No chance. Nobody knew where he had gone. I went to my minister and told him about Maggie, but I could tell he thought I was an old crazy. He gave me a big bible and actually came round one evening and prayed with me, but the only result was further punishment from Maggie, and visits from a string of Welfare Officers, Health Visitors and Social Workers the clergyman had sent to me. Let me show you something."

Mrs Fullerton fetched a large brown envelope from a drawer and handed him the contents, two sheets of A4 paper. One was headed **British Psychical Research Institution,** the other **National Society for Investigation of Paranormal Activity.** Both were reports on testings carried out at premises at 38 Trinidad Street, and the findings were remarkably similar, if couched in slightly different terms. While each commented on the 'promisingly' low atmospheric temperature, the first could find *no evidence of phenomena outside the possibilities defined by natural laws,* and concluded that *any disorder was likely to be psychogenic in nature,* while the second took *the absence of any instances of poltergeist or paranormal activity to be indicative of subjectivity of perception.*

Mrs Fullerton smiled. "I think that gobbledygook means it's all in my imagination," she remarked. "That's the same as the priest told me when I went and asked him how to apply for an exorcism. Why is it that when you get old people expect you to talk nonsense? Anyhow, I'm afraid there's nobody out there able or willing to believe, let alone help."

"So what do you think I should do?" asked Sam, conscious that the lines of approach he had been considering had already been tried and found wanting.

"Do what I had to do. Give way to her, don't displease her, learn to live with her on her terms. You can't fight her. There's no escape from her, but you learn how to make things easier for yourself. Maybe you'll be lucky like I was and be able to pass her on to somebody else."

....

Just one more to go to clear his caseload and then a couple of days of glorious freedom. He checked his file. Kynaston Court. Nice area. That was always a bonus. With the regular Health Visitor off sick he had to read up on the case record before each visit. This one looked a right bozo. His file went back eight months.

Doctor's report first: paranoia, delusion, hallucination, psychosis, schizophrenic disorder, insomnia, depression, mania. All the usual suspects. Then the Visitor's notes. Reclusive, obsessive, severe weight loss, psychological instability, growing dependency on alcohol, superstitiousness, isolation, social withdrawal, nervousness, mood swings, refusal to take medication, no suggestion of malingering. This guy had it all!

Anyhow, with a bit of luck and professional dexterity, he should have his visit to Mr Collier cleared up and written up in time for a few afternoon rounds on the golf course. Roll on the weekend.

TELL-TALE EVIDENCE

He tossed a couple of small logs on the fire, refilled his glass from the whiskey bottle, and settled back in his chair.

"You're asking me to choose one thing I'd like to be remembered for? That's a tough one. As I told you, I'm seventy eight years old, seventy eight jam-packed years, and that's a fact. It's a big span to choose from.

There is one thing that does stand out from the rest, just the same. I'll tell you about that one. I remember it as clear as a bell, as if it happened yesterday.

The strange thing is, it's one of the best and one of the worst memories that I keep inside this old head of mine. It was all over the papers at the time, and they did a whole clatter of interviews with me about it, and my photo was on television as well, but I wouldn't do an interview on the TV. Too upsetting. I have all the newspaper cuttings in a box somewhere if you want to see them.

Anyhow, I suppose the whole thing started when Gracey bought the house next door there, number 58, after old Mrs Appleton died. That was exactly twenty two years ago last month. I was still working shifts at that time down in the rail yard, so I didn't see much of my new neighbour for a few days, but I made a point of introducing myself to him over the fence on the Saturday.

The facts were simple enough. Roy Gracey had moved here from another town. He was in his forties, wasn't married, lived on his own, and was retired from work for medical reasons. It wasn't the facts that were churning over in my mind after our meeting, however, it was my first impressions of him. I've always been a good judge of people, let me tell you that. My instincts about them are never far wrong. I didn't like Roy Gracey.

All right, you're thinking it takes a bit more than one meeting over a fence to get to know a man, and maybe you're right, but, as you'll see, I'd pegged him right.

What was it I didn't like about him? For a start, setting aside the soft, wet handshake, he was far too agreeable. He was agreeing with me even before he knew the point I was making. Wasn't really interested, you see, just pretending, making the right noises, but seemed to have no real, genuine interest in the things all round him, the things going on in the real world. Phoney, you might call it.

Now that for me meant he had his own secret, inner world and, as it turned out, that was one dark, unhealthy place. OK, we all have our private thoughts and worries under the surface, health, money, relationships, any number of things, and maybe you think I was a bit hard on Gracey, but there were other things about him I didn't like. He didn't look me straight in the face the whole time we were talking. Shifty. Biting his nails all the time. Had them bitten down to the quick. I can see him now as if he was standing there in front of me, wearing the same dungarees that he had on nearly every time I saw him. Funny how you notice and remember things like that.

About six weeks after he had moved in my shift was changed so that I was at home in the afternoons. The first day of the new arrangement I happened to be looking out that small side window there behind you when I noticed Gracey crouched down among those bushes over there beside the street. It was just after three o'clock. I thought at first he was pruning the shrubs or weeding or something like that, but then I realised he was watching, waiting and watching. A few minutes later I saw why. School was out, and he was watching the kids walking home. Hidden there in the bushes he was almost within touching distance as they passed by his front garden. It was the first time I'd seen a man watching young children like that and it sent shivers through me. Weird, somehow, and scary, even though he did or said nothing, as far as I could make out. I remember seeing his face as he went back inside after the kids had passed. It looked odd, slack, his mouth drooped open in a loose kind of way.

I had no idea how long Gracey had been spying on the children but I've always believed that prevention is better than cure, so I went out front a few minutes later where he would be sure to see me and pretended to tie up some flowers. The following day, just before three, I did a bit of digging in the front bed. No sign of Gracey as the children came along. He had got the message: afternoons about three o'clock were a bad time for peeking at children from his front garden!

People in this town still talk about what happened that October. First thing anybody knew was an item on the local news about a kid gone missing, a girl of ten, from the other side of town. She had been walking home from school as usual and was last seen cutting through the neighbourhood park, same as she always did. As the days went by and the girl still missing, a series of appeals from the police and from her parents were broadcast regularly, and posters went up all over town showing her picture and asking for help from the public.

Now I might well have made a connection between the girl's disappearance and the guy living next door but for two things. First, the girl's home and school were way across town and most of the activity was concentrated there; second, and more important, Gracey had been out of town for a week or so before the girl had gone missing. His mother was ill and he was staying with her in his home town. He had told me of his proposed three week absence and had asked me to keep an eye on the place while he was away. It was one of the very few conversations we had had since his arrival.

With no clues at all about what had happened to the girl, the police called in outside help and mounted a huge door-to-door operation, checking out people's whereabouts on the day she had disappeared. They asked me about the empty house next door and I was able to tell them that the owner had been over a hundred miles away when she had vanished.

I couldn't sleep that night. Something was troubling me, niggling at my mind. I pinned it down. Why had Gracey told me he was going away? I was fairly sure he knew from the little contact we had had that I didn't like him much. It wasn't like him to approach me with information about his movements, and that business of keeping an eye on his place started to ring a bit false. He must have known with my shift work timetable that I was hardly the best person to put on guard. Was it so that I could trot out an alibi for him if it were needed?

My mind started to work overtime. <u>Was</u> he really away? <u>Was</u> he out of town? After all, days, possibly weeks, had gone by when he had been at home and I hadn't seen a sign of him. The house was just as quiet and still then when he was in it as it was now that he was supposedly out of it.

There were only three days until his scheduled return. I was tempted to call the police and get them to check out his sick mother story, but just at that point a girl answering the missing girl's description was reported to have been seen with a man in another town and all police attention was focused on following up that very strong lead. I waited for Gracey's 'return'.

It was very convincing. He arrived home in a taxi in mid-afternoon. Just the right time for me to see him, if that was what he wanted. He was carrying a suitcase. No dungarees this time, but a dark blue suit.

For a moment I felt I had got it all wrong, but I've always trusted my own instincts and they started telling me that this could easily be a charade. Gracey could have slipped out of the house at any time, perhaps stayed the night in a local hotel or boarding house, and called the taxi from there.

No, I wasn't convinced, but all I had were suspicions. I waited to see if he would play another card. He did. I teased him out by raking up the leaves on the front lawn. In no time at all he was at the fence, telling me his mother was a lot better, and thanking me for keeping an eye on things. I played my ace.

"No problem. All quiet, except one night I saw some guys in your back garden. Called the police, but it was only kids trying to steal your apples. I chased them off. No bother."

"You called the police?"

If I hadn't been watching closely I could easily have missed them, the quiver of fear in the voice and the flicker of alarm in the eyes. These were not the reactions of an ordinary concerned householder, they were the trademarks of a man with something to hide. I was more sure than ever that Gracey's story was a sham.

"Yeah, but I rang them back and told them not to bother."

Just to reinforce my suspicions, a newsflash minutes after I came back inside announced that the man and girl police had been wanting to question over the missing child had been found and eliminated from their enquiries.

The rest is history, as they say. I called the police and told them about the behaviour of the man next door. To avoid spooking him, they asked if I would go down to the station. Suddenly my evidence was the main line of enquiry, and indeed the only line of enquiry. I had made a note of the taxi company that had brought Gracey home. They traced the driver easily enough and learned that he had picked his fare up from the Meridian Hotel in the old part of the town. The hotel was able to confirm that he had stayed only one night.

Further enquiries revealed that Gracey's mother had been dead for seven years, and that Gracey had been arrested once on suspicion of exposing himself to a young girl, but the case had been dropped through lack of evidence.

The police had enough for a search warrant. I watched from the side window as they knocked on his door, two detectives, a uniformed officer, and a policewoman. Not long afterwards I saw an ambulance arriving and men in white forensic type overalls, and after that Gracey was led out handcuffed, put in one of the police cars, and driven away.

To their credit, the detectives came over here and thanked me for my information. They couldn't tell me everything, but revealed that the missing child had been found in a

....

Aaaaah. Damn. Blast."

A spark had shot out from the fire and burned his hand. He had spilt his drink as he jumped up.

A pity, and the story going so well, just getting to the climax. No point in continuing it now, the flow was interrupted. Not to worry, he'd spin a better one next evening.

He smiled to himself. How would old Gracey next door react if he knew that he had been cast as a child abductor, a paedophile? He'd probably settle for that in preference to the gay priest part he had played in Monday evening's bedtime story.

These long, lonely winter nights. Never a visitor to keep him company for an hour. Maybe some evening he would get to tell one of his tales to a real listener instead of a make-believe one.

Ah well, a couple of whiskeys and a bit of yarn spinning in front of a good fire before going to bed, there must be worse ways for a solitary old man to spend his evenings. It put the time in nicely and exercised his imagination. He'd always had a good imagination........

THE GROOM

Andy had seen enough Hotel Zora pictures in Derek's photo album and in holiday brochures that, as he now finally stood before the white stucco two storey building capped with regulation faded red tiles, he could have imagined that he was a regular guest on a return visit. Not that the Zora, apart from wisteria generously curled over doorway and ornately carved window shutters, was in any way different from dozens of other small town hotels right across Croatia. Just as Derek had predicted, it was the standardised ordinariness of everything that pleased and surprised Andy, and informed his first impressions of the country.

Andy smiled a small rebuke at himself. Something in him had been expecting bullet riddled buildings and tangled roadside wreckage, but instead all he had seen so far in this poor but proud country was the simple beauty of the place. He was no better in this respect than the tourists he sometimes met back home in Northern Ireland who were mostly relieved, but just a tiny bit disappointed, not to find war torn terrain and tanks in the streets.

Derek. Best pal from his schooldays, best man at his wedding, best friend and support when the blow had struck with such suddenness that Andy had crumpled under the shock. One moment Linda was nattering away on the phone, next moment she was lying lifeless in the hallway. Andy had never heard the phrase *cerebral aneurysm* before, or it had passed over him if he had; he afterwards wondered how something that had taken away the love of his life could have been lurking there all those happy years, a silent, anonymous enemy, one that killed with terrible efficiency.

Andy was not a religious man, but he sometimes asked himself what Linda would think or feel if she were watching him at particular moments. What would she make now of her husband standing in the square of a small, sunny town in Croatia, for the first time in his life all alone on holiday in a foreign country. Andy smiled again. She would know right away that it was Derek's doing. His words came back.

"Time's a good healer, Andy, but travel's a good nurse. It's two years now, and you need a bit of nursing. I'm going to prescribe the place Carol and I stayed last year, the place we invited you to stay with us, Konavle, near the Adriatic coastline. You owe this to yourself. Leave the details to me."

The 'details' were in the form of an Easyjet flight ticket to Dubrovnik, together with a car hire arrangement at the other end and a week's full board at the Hotel Zora. Andy was amazed how cheap the whole package was, not much dearer than a weekend in Blackpool.

He booked in with no difficulty. The man at the desk, apparently the only person in the building, seemed to be expecting him. His room, like the rest of the hotel, was plain but comfortable, and the window that opened on to the square allowed him a distant view of the surrounding low mountains, and middle distance highlands covered with vegetation. Far to the right was a thin stretch of postcard blue water dotted with shapes that he took to be small islands.

"There's a beer garden at the back, and I mean a beer garden," Derek had promised. "Not your scatter of plastic tables and chairs stuck in the back yard, but a real garden. You'll love it, Andy, you being a keen gardener. Don't get too attached, mind, there are plenty of other things to do and see."

It was a bright paradise of beauty and fragrance. Andy sat on the wooden bench and allowed the scents to assail him. One thing was certain, this garden had not been planted randomly. Whoever had chosen the shrubs and flowers had done so with care, with knowledge, and with one thing in mind above all others, perfume. Andy's nose could confidently identify white sweet rocket, nemesia, garden pinks, Moroccan broom, honeysuckle, cosmos and heliotrope, a heady mix of summer fragrances.

The Perfumed Garden. Andy smiled to himself. What was he now, fifty five? It must be forty years at least since a handful of inquisitive schoolboys had passed a well worn copy of that piece of eastern erotica round his parents' garden shed....

Andy sipped his wine and luxuriated in the colour and fragrant heat of the beer garden. Apart from an elderly German couple, he seemed to be the Zora's only guest. It pleased him to be drinking wine in a so-called beer garden. Andy had never been one for downing pints of lager. Once, and only once, he had been prevailed upon to go down to Dublin on a coach for a rugby international. In the hotel bar after the game his companions were putting away pints of Guinness and beer at an astonishing rate. When he had ordered his glass of white wine there had been a moment of stasis, with even the barman frozen for a nanosecond by the incongruity of the order.

A little Betjeman couplet slid into his mind: *Until I felt a filthy swine*
For loathing beer and liking wine.

Andy smiled at the satire and emptied his glass.

Somehow he seemed to have been doing a lot of smiling from the moment he had arrived in Croatia. He couldn't explain how, in a strange land and completely by himself, he should feel so relaxed, so at peace with himself. Whatever the reason, he felt in a more positive frame of mind now than at any time since the loss of Linda.

At first he had felt guilty about benefiting from her death. Her life insurance allowed him to retire from the bank and live in full financial security. Derek had vigorously challenged his guilt feelings.

"Look, what do you think Linda would say if you wasted all those life insurance payments? What would be the point of paying all those premiums all those years? Why take out life insurance in the first place? Knowing Linda, she would want you to use the only silver lining in the black cloud of her passing. You should feel guilty if you didn't benefit from the policy."

Andy was at his table that evening studying the menu and looking forward to the meal. The menu was in a number of languages and offered the kind of simple local food Andy preferred to the haute cuisine variety that allowed top class hotels to offer little and charge a lot. He had just settled on a main course featuring fresh fish caught locally when a figure seemed to detach itself from the back wall of the room to glide over to his table.

"Are you ready to order, sir?"

The English was perfect. The speaker had somehow managed to invest the stock question with a kind of warmth and melody. Andy asked a couple of needless questions just to hear more of the voice and see more of the waitress. She was unmistakably a local girl, with the dark hair and eyes, oval face and olive skin of her nation. She looked to be in her late twenties. Andy absently noticed that the collar and cuffs of her blouse were fringed with fine white lace. A question occurred to him.

"How did you know to speak to me in English?"

"Mystical powers," she replied, adding playfully, "which enabled me to read the Hotel Register."

"Your English is excellent, probably better than mine," returned Andy in similar light tone. "Do you mind if I ask how you speak it so well?"

"I'd be disappointed if you didn't," she laughed. "English was my main subject at university in Zagreb, and before my finals I was an exchange student for a year in Ireland, at Trinity College, Dublin. After I graduated I was English translator up north from here, in Plitvice Lakes National Park. I had to give that up when things changed at home."

During this account Andy found himself unaccountably trying to negotiate a look at the girl's wedding finger, and even more unaccountable was his relief at finally seeing the finger wore no ring.

"I'm Vedrana," the waitress concluded, as if to authenticate her narrative.

"Hello, Vedrana. I'm Andy," and they shook hands in semi-formal fashion. "Can you recommend any good drives or scenic routes for the first-time tourist?" Andy continued, neglecting to mention he had a bag full of booklets on the subject.

"Of course. I'd like you to see our lovely country at its best." Not for the first time Andy detected that note of pride when the people spoke of their nation. "May I speak with you after you have finished your meal?"

Has anyone ever set off on a holiday by himself and spent a more enjoyable opening evening? As soon as Vedrana had cleared the tables and the elderly German couple had disappeared, she rejoined Andy, bringing with her two glasses and a bottle of wine. Andy insisted upon paying for it, poured two drinks, and they touched glasses. Vedrana explained that she was filling in during the evenings for her best friend, the hotel owner's daughter, who was away in America for a month visiting her sister.

In the course of their introductory conversation Andy accidentally hit the right chord when he commented on the attractive design and content of the beer garden. Vedrana clapped her hands together with pleasure.

"It was my father Dmitar who planned and planted it. He loved flowers and plants and growing things. He was known for miles as the best gardener and landscape designer in the whole area." She raised her glass as though toasting her father's reputation.

Andy inferred that her father was dead and guessed that he had been killed in the fighting, but he knew better than to make any assumptions. A moment from his teenage years had never left him. He had been trying to chat up a girl and had somehow got the idea from talking to her that her father had died. Wanting to sound sensitive and caring he had asked, "Do you remember your dad?"

"Remember him?" the girl had cackled. "I'm trying to forget the old bugger. He ran off with the usherette from the picture house!" All her friends had overheard the exchange and a round of braying laughter followed at Andy's expense.

Andy buried his face in his glass and managed to change the subject. "Vedrana. It's a lovely name."

"Thank you. It means merry, jolly. Sometimes it's hard to live up to the name, but I do my best."

And she did, to great effect. Her year in Dublin came under review and she gave a Croatian-eye view of Dublin night life, the huge amounts spent on drink, the staggering cost of property to buy or rent, the soaring cost of living.

"I'm tellin' you the truth, sor, you could live here for a year on what you'd spend on Guinness in Dublin in a night."

A Croatian girl mimicking the Dublin brogue for a Northerner from Belfast; it was a pure delight. Where else would you get it! They started on a second bottle of wine, and Vedrana was sufficiently fortified to demonstrate some of the local dances for her guest.

She had slightly prominent front teeth, a feature that Andy had always found attractive. She was repeatedly arranging her top lip to cover them, but immediately a laugh would upset the arrangement and as the evening progressed she gave up on the attempt.

For his part, Andy could feel Vedrana studying him, assessing him, his sense of humour, his personality. Perhaps she was figuring why he was taking a holiday on his own, if he was single, divorced, widowed, or gay, but she asked no questions about his personal life and said little about her own. At some point later in the evening, however, that all changed. Perhaps the effects of the wine had taken a downturn, or her mood had simply changed, but Vedrana suddenly started to talk about her family and situation.

"We spoke about my father Dmitar earlier," she said. "He was the best man in all Croatia, the best husband and the best father. I'll never forget the phone call telling me about his accident. I was working up at the National Park. Father was pulling out tree roots on a slope near here and the tractor overturned and crushed him. He died in hospital just an hour before I got back, I didn't get to say goodbye. I had to give up my job, of course, and come home to live with mother."

The tears welled up in the dark eyes and Andy felt an almost irresistible impulse to put his arms round her, to snuggle her close. Later in his room when he examined the feeling he recognised that as well as fatherly-type comfort and basic human sympathy there was a third element, one that only the word romantic would have come close to describing.

"Is that why you never married?" he asked with genuine tenderness.

She looked up sharply. "I did marry. I was married. I'm a widow. My husband was killed in a road accident."

Andy had goofed again. What a fool. "I'm sorry. It's just that...." His voice trailed off and he was sure the flush on his face could not be blamed entirely on the wine.

"It's OK," she said, and Andy drew attention away from his discomfiture by telling her about the loss of his wife and the therapeutic reason for his holiday. She listened with real interest, the dark eyes soft and kind......

Andy slept very little his first night under the tiles of the Hotel Zora. There was a strange yet distantly familiar excitement in him, a feeling the level-headed bank official had long put behind him. The man whose daily business for thirty years had been to see that other people's hearts did not rule their heads was allowing silly, juvenile fancies to whirl about in his own.

Derek's words clamoured for attention: "You never know what's waiting down the line, Andy, what's round the corner. Put it like this, you've been the groom once and I've been your best man; if you ever want to be the groom again I'll stand beside you, and that's no disrespect to Linda."

He had arranged to meet Vedrana next morning at ten. They were going for a picnic so that she could show him the scenes and sights of her beloved homeland.

The outing was a joy from start to finish. Andy was waiting in the car in front of the hotel and when he saw her walking towards him across the tidy town square a little frisson of excitement ran though him. She was wearing a blue gingham blouse and had a red silk scarf tied round her neck, reminding Andy of the screen beauties he used to admire as a teenager on the front cover of Picturegoer.

"Your tasks today are to drive, relax, observe, and eat," she announced, patting the duffel bag she was carrying.

"And yours are to make sure I drive on the right side of the road, and don't fall asleep at the wheel," he warned in mock serious manner.

She was better than any tour guide, directing him through the valley and pointing out its traces of Roman buildings and prehistoric tumuli, before heading west towards the coast to see why Croatia is labelled the land of a thousand islands. Most of the hamlets they passed through looked identical, and the stretch of wooded hillside round each corner was indistinguishable from the previous one, but Vedrana's commentary and enthusiasm kept everything fresh and different. In truth, Andy was really more interested in the curator than in the exhibits, and was glad that Vedrana's tourist spiel was interspersed with personal material. She repeatedly referred to her father, and several times to her mother, but never to her late husband.

Andy took innumerable photos, making sure Vedrana featured in most of them 'to give perspective'. Her wit and charm and poise as he lined up the shots added fun to the sightseeing. He wondered how such a highly educated, well informed and intelligent woman could be living in relative obscurity and working as a part-time waitress. Back home she would be a top professional lady running her own company and commuting to business in a four wheel drive.

It was during the picnic that Vedrana dropped the only suggestion of a mention of her husband. She had brought a large flask of coffee and was pouring it when she casually remarked, "Maybe you would have preferred a bottle of wine."

"Definitely not, I never drink when I'm driving. With or without important passengers," he added mischievously.

Vedrana looked really pleased. It was as if he had passed a test. "I don't like men who drink and drive," she said, with total seriousness. "They destroy lives, their own and other people's."

They were on the way back to Konavle, late afternoon. Vedrana was silent and Andy could feel her looking at him. He judged it best to say nothing, to concentrate on his driving.

"Andy, will you do something for me? A favour?"

"Probably," Andy replied jokingly, but experiencing a slight fluttering in his stomach.

"I've told my mother about you and she would very much like to meet you. Would you accept an invitation to have lunch in our home, please?"

Andy had said Yes before he stopped to think what the invitation might signify, if it signified anything at all; he wished in retrospect that he knew a little more about Balkan culture and customs. Why did the word *chaperone* present itself so readily to his mind....

The meeting was arranged for Wednesday, and Andy thought it best to keep things on hold till then. In any case, a coach load of Japanese tourists had swarmed into the Zora, and Vedrana and additional staff were working full out satisfying their endless requirements. Andy drove out in the interim and, following Vedrana's directions, found her house easily. It was a modest bungalow with a profusion of flowers on one side, and a functioning vegetable patch on the other.

Andy was a little apprehensive as he walked the half mile from the hotel. Perhaps the connotations of that word *chaperone* had coloured his preconceptions, but as he knocked on the bungalow door he was expecting it to be opened by a stern faced maiden-aunt type, dressed in serious black and angular as a deckchair. Hopefully the box of chocolates he had brought would sweeten her.

How foolish did he feel when an attractive, smartly dressed woman in her late forties appeared at the door. Andy thought for a second he was at the wrong house, until he saw Vedrana immediately behind her in the hallway.

Zlata was just as bright and personable as her daughter, and had the same facial features and colouring. Andy's admiration for Vedrana grew when he discovered that she had taught her mother English, and although Zlata's delivery was halting in comparison, it was easily good enough to make communication and understanding no problem at all.

They had great amusement at Zlata's pronunciation of Andy's name. She just could not master the weak second syllable, so they happily settled for And-dee. Understandably her slight knowledge of Northern Ireland had been drawn from television reports of the Troubles, and she listened with genuine interest as he explained how huge improvements had been made in every aspect of life and living since peace and political agreement had come about. Over a glass of local wine she made intelligent comparisons between the political problems in Ireland and the Balkan States.

Andy noticed that while there were numerous photographs on display of the family - mother, daughter, and presumably father - there were none featuring someone who might have been Vedrana's husband. He steered the conversation round to his own family in the hope of shaking something loose, talking of the twins both married and living in England, and of there being no grandchildren as yet. Both women listened intently, and Zlata then lifted down one of the framed photographs and spoke of her pride in husband and daughter, but no mention at all was made of her son-in-law. It was as if he had vanished both from the earth and from their memories.

The visit that Andy had been uneasy about was one he enjoyed immensely. The meal Zlata set down was of potatoes, cabbage and peas, fresh from the garden, and a kind of spicy sausage pie which she assured him was a traditional favourite. Andy, glowing from several glasses of 'house' wine, described it with feeling to be better than anything he had tasted in years. He didn't wonder on this occasion if Linda might be watching.....

Only men who do not drink at all can truthfully claim that they have never regretted something they did or said 'under the influence'; Andy was no exception, but he could claim with equal truthfulness that he did not regret the upshot of that visit. Flushed with wine, relishing the attentions of the two women, and fairly radiating good feeling, he heard himself late in the afternoon issuing an invitation to them both to visit him in Northern Ireland, at his expense. They were overwhelmed by the offer, but were eventually prevailed upon to accept. Andy smiled privately as he pulled out Derek's 'Leave the details to me' phrase, which on this occasion meant his mailing off when he got home two return flight tickets, from Dubrovnik to Belfast International Airport…

For a variety of reasons, or feelings, none of which he could have articulated clearly even to himself, Andy chose not to tell Derek and Carol about Vedrana and his invitation. Instead he spoke generally about having met some 'nice people', and showed only the photos in which Vedrana did not appear. Nor did he mention anything of this to his twins, Hal and Evelyn, when he rang to say he was safely returned. Secrecy was part of the pleasure, the adventure.

A month after his return, a month in which he had found himself reliving his Croatian holiday over and over in his mind with the aid of the photos that featured Vedrana, Andy picked the two women up at the airport. He was in a state of suppressed excitement, and felt his mouth dry and his heart racing when they appeared at Arrivals. Hugs all round. Andy liked the old-world respect Vedrana showed in letting her mother have the front passenger seat.

"Your tasks today are to sit, observe, relax, and eat whatever delicious meals the chef sets before you," he intoned as they drove out of the airport. Vedrana laughed at the role reversal, and explained it to her mother, speaking in Croatian to make sure the full humour of the situation was conveyed. Andy's major passion besides gardening was cooking; he had planned the menus thoroughly and looked forward to showing off his culinary skills.

They stopped at a large Asda. Andy was about to dash in for an ingredient he had just thought to include, but Zlata showed such interest in the Shopping Centre that he asked if they wanted to go inside. It was like showing a child round a toy store. Zlata had never seen such a range of food and goods in her life, and she literally gazed in wide-eyed wonder as customers herded trolleys packed with purchases up and down the aisles. Andy escorted her down the mall and let her see the various shops and food outlets. He enjoyed his role as guide, especially with Vedrana watching approvingly.

Andy equally enjoyed showing his guests round his house and garden. They had a room each, the twins' former bedrooms. Both women noticed the small sliding bolts on the doors, but no comment was made. They marvelled at the size and style of the house, at the order and organisation of the garden.

That day Andy was as sparkling as the wine he poured in generous measures. He turned down all Zlata's offers to help with the meal, and proudly served 'proper' champ with gammon, minted garden peas and cauliflower cheese, followed by home-made rhubarb tart and cream. Afterwards Zlata and Vedrana seemed almost disappointed that the dishwasher exempted them from washing-up duties....

Andy was in bed. He could hear his guests chattering softly from room to room in their native tongue, and see a slit of light below his door. Next moment in the darkness he heard two bolts clicking into place and the light disappeared.

Andy had planned the next day with timetabled precision, but, after an Ulster Fry breakfast, he was so flattered by his guests' interest in himself that he took them to see the school he had attended, the bank he had worked in for over thirty years, and even the golf course he occasionally faltered round in overground hockey fashion.

The rest of the day came to heel: Mountstewart's superb sunken garden parterres, ferry to Strangford, picnic at Castleward, Castlewellan's exquisite arboretum, Seaforde's exotic butterfly garden, and the wonderful walled gardens of Rowallane. Add to these stops for ice cream and cappuccino and the programme was as packed as one day could handle.

Andy was back in the kitchen, Vedrana by his side beautiful in a turquoise top and thanking him for an unforgettable day. In deference to his guests' gastronomic experience he had skated over his personal predilection for Thai green curry, and opted for more homely shepherd's pie and apple crumble with custard. Their obvious enjoyment of the meal more than vindicated his judgement, and a second evening of flowing wine and warmth of human company found Andy as happy as the human condition will permit.

He was awake in bed. The bathroom light went off and Croatian Goodnights were softly exchanged beyond his door. Andy lay in silence, listening. There it was, one door lock clicking into place. He waited tensely for the other. Nothing. Just the blood pulsing in his temples on the pillow. Dark silence. Then something. A rustling, and brushing of door over carpet. Then the sensation of bedclothes lifting and a smooth warm naked body dovetailing in behind him.

"She is pleased with everything. She will go home in the morning. I stay as long as you want, And-dee."

BLACK & WHITE

He could have asked his mum or dad, of course, but they might have given him a soft answer, something for his own good. No, he allowed the question to gnaw at him all week until Saturday, and then, with only a slight tremble in his voice, put it to his Grandpa when they were alone together on the farm.

"Grandpa, some of the big boys in school said that the lambs are all taken away and killed. Is it true?"

Bobby omitted the terrible details the big boys had dramatised as they chased round the playground pretending to slit one another's throats. He couldn't trust his voice, and was afraid of upsetting Grandpa.

Grandpa carefully removed the cigarette from his mouth in preparation for a serious reply. It left a little white paper patch on his lower lip.

"Do you remember, Bobby, that time when we went to see Bramble being shoed? Do you remember what I said to you then?"

Bobby nodded. It was a day he would never forget: Grandpa's own favourite, Bramble the black mare, Princess Bramble, as Grandpa sometimes called her, having red hot iron shoes pressed into her feet, the clouds of smoke, the choking smell of burning that soaked into his clothes and stayed with him all day, and then those squared nails being driven into poor Bramble's hooves. Bobby had burst into tears as the cruel man hammered and filed and pared with his strong veiny arms and huge hands.

Grandpa had instantly noticed his distress and lifted him up level with Bramble's head so that he could see his own face reflected in the large liquid black eyes.

"Bobby, give her a pat. Rub her ears. There now, does she look sore, does she look in pain, or does she look proud of her new shoes?

You see, Bobby, Bramble trusts me, she knows I would never do anything to hurt her. You're never made to suffer by the ones who love you."

The words came back to Bobby now as Grandpa lifted him high and set him on the top bar of a gate. They made sense. Would his own mum and dad make him suffer terrible pain? He felt immediately comforted. The lambs were safe.

Bobby loved all the animals on the farm, but it was the lambs he loved best of all, their hard little butting heads, their wiggling tails as they guzzled their mothers, their jumping and prancing and incessant high-pitched bleatings. It always saddened him when he would arrive at the farm to find some of them had been taken away.

"What does happen to the lambs, Grandpa, when they go away in the big lorry?"

"Well, they get too big for me to look after here, so they have to go to a bigger farm to grow to full size, and then they get all their long wool cut off to make lovely woollen clothes to keep poor people warm in winter."

Bobby liked the explanation. Those horrible boys at school were telling lies. Or maybe somebody had told them lies. They mustn't have a Grandpa like he had to tell them the truth. His heart swelled with gratitude for having such a Grandpa.

No wonder he looked forward all week to the Saturday visit to the farm. The first Grandpa hug he got on arrival was scented with tobacco and woodshavings and ropes and hay and horsey smells. Then came the paper bag full of sweets that looked like marbles and tasted a little like cough mixture. Then, best of all, the animals: calves with sticky tongues, wriggling pink piglets, countless tabby kittens, and, of course, the funny, furry lambs.

"I love you, Grandpa," Bobby suddenly blurted out, and as he threw his arms round him to be lifted down from the gate, he noticed the eyes that were looking down at him were moist. Not for the first time Bobby was mystified by the way grown-ups cried just as much when they were happy as when they were sad or hurting.

They were on the way back home in the car, always a perfect end to the day. Bobby would lie on the soft seat in the back and listen to the road purring, mile after mile, until he fell asleep. Normally he would half-waken as his dad was carrying him into the house, but he would be too sleepy to do more than simply allow himself to be put into bed.

"It's all that good fresh country air tires him out," his mum would usually remark as she tucked him in.

This journey was different. Bobby was indeed lying with his eyes closed, but his mind was wide awake with the happiness of the day. The lights of passing cars were orange through his eyelids and whenever he opened them he could see the dark silhouetted shapes of his dad and mum in the front.

Suddenly he found himself listening to their conversation. The words were low and serious and clear. They were talking about Grandpa, in the same way they sometimes spoke about Bobby when they thought he was asleep or not listening. They spoke as if Grandpa needed looking after and protected, instead of being someone who knew everything and could do and make anything.

Bobby could not understand many of their anxious words, big words, strange words, but he recognised enough, *hospital, doctor, treatment,* to understand that Grandpa was sick. It was what came next that set Bobby's heart pounding and ruined all the happiness of the day.

"It'll break his heart getting rid of all the animals, but there's no other way. When he gets out he'll be in no state to look after himself, let alone all that stock. They'll have to go to the slaughterhouse. Poor dad, he'll be lost without something to feed and look after. That's been his whole life. The place will be quiet without them."

In the darkness Bobby thought about his Grandpa and how sad he would be losing his lovely Princess Bramble and all the other animals. A terrible thought hit him: maybe the lambs **did** go to the slaughterhouse, maybe the big boys were right after all about what happened to them, and poor Grandpa had been lied to with those stories of big full-grown lambs and woollen clothes. It could have been the bad men who came in the lorry to take them away who lied to him. Bobby felt his eyes fill with tears.

Grandpa mustn't find out about Bramble and the animals. He mustn't find out the truth. Bobby would protect him. If you loved somebody, you wouldn't let him suffer. It was up to him to see that Grandpa was protected from suffering.

Bobby allowed himself to be carried into the house and made ready for bed. Just as his mum was about to turn out the light he sat up.

"Mum, is it always wrong to tell lies? Didn't you say that it's sometimes all right?"

She looked at her kind-hearted boy and saw the gentleness of her father in his dark, serious eyes, so that she had to struggle to make her reply.

"Bobby, it's nearly always better to tell the truth, but sometimes you can tell a white lie.

What that means is hiding the truth if it is going to hurt somebody who doesn't deserve to be hurt. You only tell white lies to those you like or love."

Grandpa looked so strange in the hospital bed and had changed so much in the three weeks since Bobby had seen him on the farm that for a few moments it was like seeing a different person. The old rough tweed jacket had given way to silly looking pyjamas, and instead of lengths of coarse twine dangling from his pockets there were pipes and tubes attached to his arms and protruding below the sheets. His face brightened when he saw Bobby.

"Bobby, Bobby, and how's my best boy? Come up and see your old Grandpa."

Bobby couldn't wait to tell him the good news. "Grandpa, you'll never guess who I saw. Bramble. Princess Bramble. She's in a field of grass thick with clover, and she has two or three other nice horses for company. I stroked her and although she's missing you, she's really happy."

As Bobby breathlessly finished his report he noticed that same wetness once again in his Grandpa's eyes and he knew, knew for sure, that they were tears of happiness, put there by his white lie about the black mare.

THE WINNER

The last twist of the knife, a fourth goal conceded right on the final whistle. Jake watched his team troop disconsolately off the pitch, and then joined the handful of regulars shuffling into the Club Room. It struck him, as it did every Saturday, that while he was sunk in frustration and disappointment at yet another defeat, the other supporters were already exchanging the ritual after-match banter and wisecracks. Win or lose, the result seemed to make no difference to them.

In this, if in nothing else, Jake envied them. He knew he could never accept defeat with that kind of indifference. No, Jake was a brooder, a bad loser. What kind of a winner he might be was still undetermined. Only a few weeks away from the big Four O, and there was nothing, absolutely nothing, in all those years that he could look back on as a success, let alone a triumph.

As his Guinness swirled muddily into its glass behind the bar counter, Jake felt familiar black thoughts clouding into his head and darkening his mind. They oppressed him now on a daily basis, like a heavy mass, crouching over every part of his being, past and present, and obscuring any faint glimmer of hope for the days ahead.

He mechanically lowered his drink a few inches and stared into its thick darkness. As he raised the glass for a second swig, he caught his reflection in the mirror on the back wall behind the bar optics and glass shelving. Where once he might have seen a young man with dreams of love, wealth, happiness, there now squatted a loser, a man in a loveless marriage, in debt, in a dead-end job, in a rented house, in middling health, in middle age, and in the club room of a team that hadn't won a match since early September.

Add to this record last month's diabetes diagnosis, the recent row at work that had lost him the only friend he had, and a profoundly deaf son who lived away all week in a Special School, and there was Jake Duddy's scoresheet to date, as well as a forecast of results to come.

Jake joylessly finished his pint, thought about another one, nodded to the group watching the over-coloured race meeting on the large screen TV, and pushed out into the rawness of a December late afternoon.

His mind scanned ahead: he hoped Madge would be in the kitchen when he got back. He would go straight into the front room for the results, and avoid having to speak to her. The sound of her voice was now enough to set his nerves on edge.

There had been a time when she would joke that she knew the match result by the look on his face, but there were no jokes between them now, and it wasn't because his team could be depended on to lose every week. In any case, even if by some miracle they were to win a match, Jake doubted if his face could now assume any expression other than its regular fixed scowl. It was true what he had overheard said about him one week in the club: "Jake looks as if he's always facing into the wind."

Madge. He couldn't shake her loose from his thoughts. The numbing truth was that he found her repulsive, he could hardly bear to look at her, let alone touch her. Her psoriasis had flared up again, worse than ever, covering her scalp as well as her arms and hands and legs. Also back was the recurrent cold sore on her lower lip that left her mouth pink and puffy, like a lump of well used bubblegum. A tiny little voice told Jake that he should be feeling sympathy for Madge, but all he could honestly recognise in himself were feelings of disgust and revulsion.

It was something else on the domestic front, however, that troubled him far more deeply than his thoughts about Madge. It concerned his son. Whenever Jonny came home at the weekends from the School, sometimes bringing a friend or two to stay over, he was always alive with the things they had done, the places they had been, the people they had met. So much was done for the students: there seemed to be a continuous round of outings, dances, concerts, parties, visits, sports. As Jake absorbed the exciting social life his eighteen year old son was enjoying, any parental feelings of pride and pleasure were swept over by a dark tide of envy and resentment. Appalling it might be, unnatural, unforgivable, but Jake was jealous of his own handicapped son…. He shuddered and tightened his scarf round his face as the cold wind sliced between the stark rows of houses, and the streetlights came flickering on.

Madge was steadily ironing in the kitchen. She heard Jake come in, and the TV go on.

She sighed aloud, a habit she had developed. Jonny wasn't coming home this weekend. He was going to Aviemore for skiing lessons.

Madge looked forward all week to his return at the weekends. Jonny was the one good thing in her life. All her love, her soft feelings, she gave to him. He deserved them. He was such a good-hearted, sweet-tempered boy. It was as though nature had in this way compensated him for his disability.

Madge smiled as she folded the clothes, even though she knew there would be no relief this weekend from her husband's cold, relentless bitterness. At least she had one breath of happiness in the smothering gloom of her marriage.

She was just finishing the last shirt when, without warning, the door burst open and Jake was there right in front of her. Madge knew at once that something was wrong, terribly wrong. He was standing looking right at her, and he was *smiling*. No, worse than that, more terrifying, he was making the half-choked guffawing sounds that she remembered from way back as her husband's form of laughing. Something else was wrong. His posture. The beaten man's hunch was gone, he was standing upright.

"Jake, what's wrong? What is it? Are you OK?"

Madge's belief that he had suffered some kind of brainstorm was confirmed the next moment when he said, "Madge," before clamping his hand over his mouth to imprison another guffaw. Jake hadn't called her by name for two years or more. Next thing, to the accompaniment of strangled chortlings, he took her by the hands across the ironing table. All doubt was gone, he had definitely flipped.

She was wondering whether to phone the doctor or run next door for help, when he burst out in a kind of sob, "Madge, Madge, I've done it. I can't believe it, I've done it. I've hit the big one. You're not going to believe this. I've won the pools. We're rich. Twenty three points, Madge, twenty three points, the big one, seven score draws and a no score, and I've got the lot. Madge, Madge, d'you know what this means, twenty three, seven threes and a two, the big one. Claims required for twenty three points. Dividend forecast excellent."

Drunk with joy, Jake repeated the winning formula several more times, adding details of complicated lines and perms that meant nothing to her, and were more of an attempt to confirm for himself the reality of his success. Abruptly he glanced at his watch and ushered Madge into the front room in time to catch the results on the other channel. His hands were trembling as he checked the numbers against his copy coupon, shouting 'Yes' with each draw, and making doubly sure by matching them again with the list of draws shown at the end of the results broadcast. There was no doubt about it, Jake had scooped the jackpot.

Excitement coursed through him like an electric current. "I told you, Madge, I told you, I always said I'd win the big one." Caught up in the euphoria, she didn't point out his lament every Saturday afternoon as he tossed the coupon in a ball into the fire: *No chance. What's the use? Waste of time. Me win anything? I'm a born loser, a beaten docket.*

Jake didn't know yet how much he had won, or if there were any other winners, but he was certain that it was a matter of hundreds of thousands, possibly a million or more. He kept sitting down and getting up again, talking non-stop, and at moments seemed almost on the verge of tears.

The win and its ramifications liberated a frenzy of mixed thoughts and feelings in him. As well as the obvious satisfaction of telling that little poisonous Welsh git of a boss what he could do with his job, and the delirious visions of new car, big house, and similar material possessions, Jake discovered gentler fancies stealing into his mind, the kind of considerations he hadn't entertained in years. Among them were the most expensive treatments for poor Madge's skin disease, and the best private specialists to examine Jonny's hearing condition. How can money be the root of all evil when it can kindle such worthy intentions….

Jostling for space too, however, were darker notions. Jake regretted having ticked the No Publicity box, but he'd make sure just the same that everybody knew of his glorious win. There were a few in particular whose faces he'd love to see when they heard Jake Duddy had won a million or more.

Derek Gooding! Derek Gooding! Yes, yes, yes, Derek Gooding. Jake had hated him all the way up through school, especially when Gooding had gone on to university and higher things.

That little moment a few months back jagged him again. Jake had been downtown and had chanced to look into the smart restaurant beside his bus stop. There in his flash suit, and in the company of a stunning young woman, sat Gooding, his dark red wine glass raised, his laundered white plumage glowing in the candlelight. He looked up and must have seen Jake because there was a self-satisfied smirk on his face. Jake shuddered now in anticipation as he envisaged Gooding's response to the news of his big win……

Tender sentiments returned as he watched Madge fold away the eternal ironing board. He rose to a joke. "Madge, it's the end of the Iron Age, it's the Golden Age now for the Duddy family."

Madge looked up with tears in her eyes, her poor face strangely pretty behind the reddish patches. "It's scary. What happens now?"

What happens now? How many times he had fantasised about precisely that. He did so again, only this time it was no fantasy, it was for real. Another spasm of excitement quivered right through him, and he snorted through his nose in his efforts to subdue a triumphant laugh.

He spread his copy coupon on the telephone table in the hall, took a deep breath, and with a hand that shook a little in spite of his best efforts, dialled the familiar number.

"Littlewoods Pools Office. May I help you?"

"Yes, I've got twenty three points on this week's coupon." Jake's voice was controlled, apart from the slight tremor when he got to the second syllable of the last word.

"Thank you, sir. Could I have your name and address, your reference number, which you'll find in a little box at the bottom of your coupon, and the Agency reference, if there is one filled in on the coupon."

Jake gave her the information, aware of the contrast between her level professional tone and his own unsteady delivery. He tried a wink to Madge, who was cowering in the corner as though afraid of the enormity and speed of events.

"Thank you. Just hold the line for a moment and I'll be right back to you."

Most people have at least one defining moment in their lives, an instant that shapes or colours the remainder of their existence, or their perception of it. For Jake Duddy that moment was expressed in nine flat words that reached him next down a telephone line:

"We are not in receipt of your coupon, sir."

For a second the import of the words was delayed, but when it struck the effect was the same as if Jake had jumped into a pool of ice cold water. His breath was sucked out of him, his stomach was a vacuum, his legs were rubber. How he managed to articulate a reply he could never have explained.

"But you must have got it. I posted it myself, first class, on Thursday morning."

"There's no mistake on our part, sir. Our system guarantees that."

Jake spluttered some irrelevant details about exactly how and where and when he had posted his coupon, but the woman was totally confident that it had not been received. She had the manner of someone trained to deal with drunks, cranks, losers.

"We'll check it again if you wish, sir," she finished, "and call you back if anything shows up." Her tone said that nothing was going to show up.

Jake's head was a whirlpool of bewilderment, disappointment, rage. He kept repeating, again and again, "There must be some mistake. I posted it myself on Thursday morning. I posted it myself, out at New Meadows. I dashed through the rain and posted it myself. They must have got it. There must be some mistake."

But there was no mistake. Jake controlled his rising despair and trembling hands enough to ring back, and was informed by a different woman, "There are no jackpot winners this week."

It was true. All his dreams were gone, his big moment was in ruins. But why? How? He had definitely posted the coupon first thing on Thursday morning on his way to work. In confusion, in bitter self-pity and wretchedness of mind, Jake felt his head was going to explode. It used to be when he was drunk and everything was whirling he could close his eyes and wait for the dizziness to decrease, but this was worse, a hundred times worse. Instead of reducing, the terrible giddiness was intensifying until he really felt his brain was going to burst.

Madge was sobbing steadily in the corner, perhaps in sympathy for him or for herself, or from a more general sorrow, but Jake wasn't even aware of her presence. How long he had waited for some kind of success, some stroke of good fortune, and now to have it cruelly torn away from him. And what were the odds of a repeat, a second chance: if it was about a million to one hitting the jackpot once, the odds against Jake filling again were astronomical, incalculable. He might as well pack in the whole thing. Why had he believed for a moment that luck had smiled on him, when the evidence of his entire life marked him out as a no-hoper.

Just at the point when he felt the boiler of his mind was about to blow, an emergency valve mercifully opened to release the bursting pressure. The Post Office! That's where the fault lay, with the Post Office. That's who had robbed him of everything, that's where he would find his target. The blessed relief of rage. It didn't reduce the pounding in his head, but it redirected its force into a savagery against the public service that had left his hopes in ruins.

Jake was at the head of the small queue outside the main post office on Monday morning. His headache was that of a man who hadn't slept for two nights and who doubted if he would ever enjoy a peaceful night's sleep in his life again, but there was now a focus and desperate determination that kept his inner tumult under control.

By a tremendous effort of will Jake suppressed his anger sufficiently to explain to the woman behind the counter what had happened. With her wrenched-back hair and prominent front teeth, she looked for all the world like Bugs Bunny. She listened carelessly to Jake's accusations, unimpressed by the enormity of the delivery failure and its consequences for the sender. This was not what she wanted from her first customer first thing on a Monday morning.

When Jake had finished his arraignment of the entire Post Office system, the woman wrinkled her nose, and started to 'rabbit' on about first and second deliveries, and compensation up to £30 and £500. What was the stupid bitch talking about, hadn't she heard that he had lost a million pounds or more by the negligence of her organisation?

"So," the recital finished, "if you didn't send it Recorded Delivery or Registered Post, all we can do is put a trace on it."

Jake was spluttering with impatience and frustration. "Is putting it in the box not good enough any more? Is the Post Office not responsible for looking after and delivering people's mail? Is New Meadows some kinda backwoods, or something?"

The rabbit stiffened. "New Meadows? I'm sorry, sir, but if you posted your item in our New Meadows sub branch, you'll have to make your enquiry there. The trace will have to be put on from there." Her tone said that her part in the case was now terminated.

Jake wanted to throttle and possibly skin the creature, but he swallowed hard and told her how he had posted his coupon in a post box, not in the sub post office.

"Post Box? What Post Box? There is no post box at New Meadows, and I should know, sir, for I happen to live at New Meadows, and have done for thirty years. I'm sorry, sir, but you're mistaken. Next."

Jake's protestations were to no avail, and he stumbled home in a fury so strong that it almost supplanted his distress at having lost a fortune. He dragged Madge into the car. "No post box, no post box? She'll need to do better than that before I'm finished with her. Does she know who she's dealing with?"

The tirade continued all the way out to New Meadows, Madge crouched in the back seat in silent misery. Jake finally pulled up in front of a bright red Post Office box sunk in a newly-built curved brick wall.

Even as he was pointing it out to Madge, Jake realised his mistake. There was no lettering on the postbox, no times of collection, no public information. What he was looking at, what he had entrusted his precious coupon to, was a household letter box set into a private garden wall.

A sickness overwhelmed him at the moment of discovery, and another army of terrible thoughts started to batter his beleagured brain.

"That's not a post box, Jake," came a small voice from the back. "That's somebody's letter box. Look, there's a big GR in gold. It's an antique one. I'm surprised you didn't notice that."

It was the closest Madge would come to blaming him outright, but Jake noticed a hint of satisfaction in her voice. The truth reached him in that instant. Madge hated him. His wife hated him. In his despair Jake almost welcomed the revelation, like a man cast down beyond hope perversely invites the pain of further misfortune.

If only he had left things as they were. Jake used to leave his coupon each week with the shopkeeper on the corner who acted as a pools Agent, but when the shop was robbed a few months earlier and cleared of most of its stock, Jake decided it was too risky to continue the practice, and started sending off the coupons himself. If only, if only. And now who could he blame but himself. He was utterly alone in his suffering, nobody cared, not even his family, and it was all down to his own mistake. Yes, it had been raining and he had raced from the car and thrust the envelope into the box, and it was, after all, a post box originally, but the fault still lay with him.

"It's not fair," he cried out loud with the helpless passion of a child, " how was I to know the difference? They shouldn't allow these things to be used as letter boxes. And look at me, look what's happened to me."

Jake was almost in tears, at the bottom of the pit, when suddenly, for the second time, in the midst of his desperate grief, the lifeline of anger was thrown to him. Of course, of course! Why hadn't the bastard who owned the letter box not posted his coupon on! That's what should have happened. If he had had any decency at all, he should have posted it on. Jake didn't stop to ask himself if he would have behaved decently in the same circumstances. No, his frantic mind was off and running on a new scent, the victim this time an easier one, an individual instead of a government body.

His reeling brain steadied. He had it. He would go home, get himself resettled, recharged, ready for battle, and next morning bright and early he would present himself at the door of the hated householder, and let justice take whatever form it chose.....

The cold winter sunlight slanted into the room and lit the sleeping man's pillow. It was enough to waken him. Although he had driven home dog-tired straight from the airport, he had slept badly, probably owing to a combination of jet-lag and mental activity.

Yes, it had been a hectic five-day visit to Boston, but a hugely successful one, and he was back with a diary stuffed with useful names, and a briefcase containing three actual black and white deals. What was it that wealthy old Bostonian had said to him: a contact is only one letter away from a contract. Neat.

He stretched and looked out of the bedroom window. The new driveway was a good job, and, apart from a couple of little thin patches, the lawn had taken well.

His next look was ahead. First a glass of orange juice, followed by a cup of the coffee he had brought home with him, and then a couple of lengths in the inside heated swimming pool. After that he'd need to go down and collect his mail at the Post Office. Oh yes, he'd check to make sure nobody had mistaken his private letterbox for the real thing, as had happened a few times just after the wall and pillars were finished; he had been quick to post the letters on immediately, not wishing to inconvenience any of his new neighbours.

Then before lunch the triumphant appearance at the office with the captures he'd made in the States. He could hardly wait. He stretched again, a stretch of satisfaction. Yes, life was good for Derek Gooding, a man at ease with himself and at peace with all the world.....

THE MARK

Looking back now on that first year at Art College, with the perspective of time and distance, I suppose I can see some shape and order in it, although at the time everything seemed totally hectic. Not much turned out the way I had hoped or planned, but I learned a little about art and a lot about life. I also formed indelible impressions and memories, especially within our group of three.

It was College that alphabetically formed our Graham, Greaves and Halliday unit, for simple administrative purposes. The triumvirate proved, during its brief lifespan, to be an eminently successful combination in that the human and social chemistry among the three of us, apparently against the odds, worked very satisfactorily indeed.

I was Greaves, the middle one placed between two polar opposites, and it was right that I should have been in central position. I was of unremarkable personality, average ability and moderate opinion, preferring to be the critic in the audience rather than the player on the stage.

It was equally right that Tony Graham should have come first alphabetically because he occupied first place in almost every other regard, the exceptions being social and financial standing. If a figure had been needed to represent the archetypal Art student, then Tony would have fitted the bill. He was thin and pale, with brooding David Essex type good looks; paradoxically he suggested both vulnerable sensitivity of nature and maverick independence of mind and thought.

I can still remember clearly my very first chat with him on our induction day. I had been boring him with a recital of my hopes and ambitions for my Art College career, and finished, "I'm here simply to see if I'm good enough to deserve to be here."

"I'm here strictly from hunger," said Tony.

I didn't know how to react, not being quite sure what he meant, and not knowing him well enough to read the tone. The same was true when we met up on Monday morning, and I casually asked him if he had had a good weekend.

"I met a man who made me laugh, I met a girl who made me cry," came the reply.

What a poser, what a phoney, what a pretentious prat! These were my instant feelings. Later when I got to know him closely I found I had misjudged him. This theatricality of speech was no affectation, but one element of Tony Graham's indefinable, contradictory identity. Tony didn't fit into any of the usual boxes: the penniless art student in his lonely garret, the flamboyant bohemian rollicking in the pub, the flawed artistic genius wrestling his personal demons. The fascinating feature of his character was that he could defy such stereotypes, be a likable, essentially decent person, and yet remain such a different, interesting, enigmatic, individual.

It took me some time to reach these conclusions. One of my many weaknesses is a tendency to want to pigeon-hole people.

The third member of our band of three was Gareth Halliday. I honestly did sometimes think of myself as the fulcrum in the middle of a set of scales, with Tony and Gareth counterbalancing each other on either side. It also struck me at some point that if I was ever called on to give a description of Gareth, all I needed to do was think of half a dozen words to describe Tony and come up with their opposites.

Beyond saying that Gareth had no artistic ability whatever, and even less personality, I'm not going to list the series of neutrals and negatives that would stack up. The one quality that he did have in common with Tony was a basic good-heartedness, not that anyone bothered enough with him to recognise it, or benefit from it. The extraordinary thing was that Tony and Gareth, the chalk and the cheese, the day and the night, actually got on very well and genuinely seemed to like each other.

All three of us had one thing in common. The first year, the Foundation Studies year, introduced us to three options, painting, sculpture or graphic design; each of us was determined at the end of it to choose painting.

"That's what my dad wants me to do," explained Gareth. "I scraped in with my A level grades in Art and History and Appreciation of Art. Don't know how, or why, but that's what he wants me to do."

"You're looking good," said Tony. "Damien Hirst got an E," and we all laughed.

Right from the opening day Tony exhibited the eccentric behaviour that set him almost irretrievably apart from his fellow students and from the life of the College. While the rest of us on that first morning negotiated our way about the campus, or arranged to meet our tutors or lecturers, he located the 'Quartermaster's Store', as it was called, and set about buying practice materials at the special reduced price available for registered students. When we bumped into him by chance about an hour later, he was carrying a cardboard box crammed with paints, brushes, canvases, sketch pads and other art materials.

Gareth and I thought this was unusual, of course, but neither of us had any idea at that particular moment that even more unusual was Tony's being there at all. We simply assumed that we would be seeing him every day. In the event, sightings of Tony Graham at the Art College came to be as rare and talked-about as glimpses of the Yeti in the Himalayas. He attended no lectures or tutorials, was assigned to no projects or modules of study, produced no written or practical work, and took no part in any aspect of College life, social or otherwise.

On those rare occasions when he did put in an appearance, he was accompanied by one or more silent-movie type girls, thin and white faced, with dark eyes and hair, and wrapped in black dresses or coats. At first we thought they might have been Tony's sisters, so alike were they to him in their frail, attractive, interesting appearance, but by the time we had met about four or five of this satellite sorority, we figured they must be girl friends or girlfriends. If I had taken any of them home, I was certain, the first thing my mother would have done would have been to set them down to a good meal.

Amusingly, Tony's appearances, or lack of them, became for a short spell a kind of byword for improbability in our class of first year students. I remember overhearing two of the girls in the canteen: "Have this essay finished by the weekend? I've more chance of seeing Tony Graham."

Gareth and I were possibly the only two who noticed that his very infrequent visits always ended with a cardboard box stuffed with newly purchased art materials. We definitely were the only two students who saw him on a regular basis. Our meetings took place in The Eager Elbow pub on Market Street. He arranged the first meeting that opening day, and thereafter we would arrange the next one before we left the pub. Why exactly he wanted to maintain contact with us we were never quite sure. My feeling now is that he was probably lonely, nothing more mysterious than that, but back then such an idea would never have entered my mind.

All we knew was that he was the embodiment of elusiveness, and not just on account of his absences from College. Even when we were with him we couldn't quite pin him down, read his mood, follow his thinking, predict his reactions.

I can see him now as clearly as if it were yesterday, hunched inside his dark overcoat, rolling a cigarette and sipping his black coffee. At first we had assumed he was rolling joints, but we soon learned that he didn't do drugs at all. Likewise he drank only occasionally, a glass or so of red wine on special occasions. The rumours among our peers that Graham was a dope addict and/or alcoholic sounded downright silly to students Greaves and Halliday, but we could see how they would have arisen. Tony Graham fitted exactly the popular picture of a druggie drop-out, and his aberrant behaviour supported that assumption. The odd thing was that although it was open season on Tony for the critics, neither Gareth nor I ever heard him make any kind of disparaging personal remark about college staff, students, or indeed anyone else.

Another assumption, this one made only by Gareth and me, was that he was a seriously good artist. This was certainly not based on any work we had seen, but it somehow never occurred to us that he would not be. We asked him from time to time what he was doing all those weeks he should have been with us at College, and when he replied each time that he was 'working on something' we automatically believed it to be something good, even great. From our point of view, the one positive in Tony's continuous absence from classes was that it spared us the embarrassment of his seeing our stuff. An added consolation for me was that however poor my painting might be, it was never going to reach the depths consistently displayed in Gareth's.

We tried to encourage Tony to put in an occasional appearance at a lecture or tutorial, or present a piece of work as a token of intent. From what he told us about the warnings he was receiving from the college authorities, some compromise on his part was becoming increasingly necessary.

About the beginning of December we met up as usual in the pub, and somewhere in the course of the conversation Gareth suddenly asked Tony and me if we would accept an invitation to his house for a meal. Without hesitation Tony said he would be honoured, and I swung in behind his acceptance.

"Great," said Gareth, "great. My dad will be really pleased."

The Hallidays lived in Morston, the posh area of town. Gareth, one of the few students in those days to own a car, drove us out in his Triumph Herald.

The evening was a great success. Apart from the predictable style and grandeur of the house itself, it was also an evening of surprises. Gareth Halliday was a large-framed, hefty young man, and I had unconsciously been expecting that his father would be a man built on a similar scale, but, like his wife, he was a small, slightly made figure in advanced middle age. Gareth, their only child, had, as his mother told us during the course of the evening, 'arrived late'.

What interested me was how Tony would react to this affluent, comfortable middle class milieu. Would the artist despise its bourgeois values and easy life-style? Of course he wouldn't, and didn't. I was the only one who considered it for a moment. Tony showed respect as he listened to how Mr Halliday had started with nothing and built up a small chain of grocery stores. I think perhaps he admired the strength of will and independence behind the success.

"Yes, I was lucky, the big superstores were just starting to appear on the horizon when I decided I'd done enough and sold the lot. I couldn't compete nowadays, in any case. The small retailer is dead and gone. I got out just in time before they buried me."

As the meal was served and wine generously poured, it emerged that Mr Halliday, now that he was retired and financially secure, wanted something more from life. He was interested in the arts and culture and good taste. I began to see why Gareth had been propelled into Art School. As a friend, and presumably as a son, he was compliant to a fault, ready at the drop of a hat to follow others' lead with the energy and single-mindedness of a gun dog. I'm convinced that if his father had wanted him to be an accountant or a blacksmith, he would have pursued either career with equal assiduousness.

As for Mr Halliday, he was at the stage where he was wanting to buy, eager to buy, but afraid of not knowing what to buy. Like Gareth, he was without guile, and openly declared his position.

"For a man my age, I'm a complete beginner at these things. I'd like to own good works of art, not as an investment or anything like that, but just to have them for their own sake. The problem is that I don't trust my own judgement, I don't know what's good and what isn't."

A silence followed this confession, nobody wanting to presume to instruct our host on that most subjective and contentious of subjects, good taste. The expectation round the table was that Tony would be the one to respond. He lifted his glass of Merlot and studied it close to a glowing candle.

"This is a lovely wine. I like the look of this wine. It makes me want to know it better, to allow it to work on me, give me pleasure and, no doubt, some pain, unsettle me, influence my thoughts and mood and feelings. A man should enjoy being led astray by good wine. That's the power of what I'm looking at in this glass. I'm no wine connoisseur, but for me, this is good wine."

The meal was over, everyone was a little drunk, and we were sampling richly coloured liqueurs. The world of canteen sandwiches and vending machine coffee seemed a distant place.

"Gareth, why don't you show the boys your place upstairs," suggested his mother.

The place must once have been a large bedroom at the back of the house. It had now been converted into the standard artist's studio, with no expense spared. All the accoutrements were there: easels, canvases, hardboard, all manner of paper and cardboard sheets and pads, paints of every variety in their respective tubes and pots, box after box of charcoals and chalks and conte crayons, enough brushes to supply the College for a year, and shelves laden with books on every kind of art and artist. Gareth's studio could have given the Quartermaster's Store a run for its money.

The owner seemed a little embarrassed by the excesses of his stock. Perhaps, like me, he was thinking of Tony's cardboard boxes and their cut price contents.

"Don't know why you bother going into College, Gareth," I remarked facetiously. "Why don't you arrange for the tutors to come out here to you? Better working conditions in a superior location."

Tony meantime was walking round inspecting the goods on display. The only thing missing was evidence of any painting having been done. To the left of the doorway was an expanse of virgin white wall. Tony suddenly picked up a stick of charcoal and, while we watched, wrote up this odd little verse that has stayed in my mind all these years.

> *I am Art,*
> *I live for ever,*
> *my father inspiration*
> *my mother imagination.*
> *I wither never,*
> *I grow in the heart.*

He set down the charcoal, opened a pot of red paint, selected a brush, and with one effortless sweeping flourish described a swirling arabesque design underneath. It was a perfect creation, the work of seconds, flawless in the execution of its graceful curving lines and fading tail. It was the signature of artistry.

"The artist should make his mark in society," said Tony with a strange little self-deprecatory and yet self-assured laugh, an uncharacteristic laugh that the wine must have prompted. The next time I saw that motif on the wall of Gareth's studio it was surrounded with literally dozens of imitations. Gareth had copied, traced, duplicated, reproduced Tony's mural design by every possible means, and not one of them had the same *first fine careless rapture* of the original. In fairness, I have to add that on a later viewing all the copies had been painted over and only Tony's original words and artistic postscript had been spared…..

We were a few weeks into the second term and the expulsion warning light was flashing red for Tony. Gareth and I were in the canteen when one of his silent-screen females suddenly appeared. She had looked us out to deliver two envelopes.

"Tony sends his apologies for not being able to give you these himself, but he's very busy."

We offered her a coffee in the hope of hearing something about him from a third party, but she declined and melted away into the crowd.

The envelopes contained an invitation. I still have my one, sitting in front of me right now.

You are invited to the opening of
STREETLIGHT
an exhibition of paintings by
Tony Graham
in The Loft Gallery, Sugar Lane
Thursday 1st February, 7.45pm

The invitation was home-made, typed on a piece of thin card. Neither Gareth nor I had heard of The Loft gallery, nor did we know where Sugar Lane was, but we quickly ascertained that it was an alley off Tabard Street in what had been the old docks area of the town. From our limited knowledge of the district, it seemed an odd place to find an Art Gallery.

We found the alley easily enough, but could easily have missed the exact location had Gareth not spotted an arrow, tied to a lamp post, with the legend *Loft Gallery* handprinted along its length. The arrow pointed to a doorway serving a small café, with a steep wooden stairway running up the left side. At the top of the second flight, pinned above a door, was another notice in the same print and bearing the same title. The lettering was unmistakably Tony's. He told us later that he had rented the loft from the café owner beneath and that its life as an Art Gallery had started that morning and would finish at the end of a week.

I couldn't help drawing a contrast between the simple expedients and economy used here to effect a change of use and the extravagance of effort and money needed to create Gareth's studio.

The room itself was long and low with a sloping roof. A small table just inside the door offered typed sheets with a list of the paintings on display. Apart from the four Lillian Gish lookalikes in a small group at one end, and a couple of down-and-outs shuffling aimlessly about, Tony had nobody but Gareth and me to see his work.

He looked frail and worn out, but was genuinely pleased to see us and welcomed us warmly. I can still see his breath in the bitingly cold February air that had found its way upstairs from the bare streets below. One of the girls slid away from the small cluster and handed us glasses which she filled with deep red wine. Unless I'm mistaken, it was the same Merlot that he had commended some weeks earlier in a very different setting.

I'm surprised that I can remember these small details from an evening that was unlike anything that I'm likely to experience again. I don't know if every man has in his lifetime one transcendental moment or occasion, probably not, but for me, and for Gareth too, that visit to Tony's humble exhibition introduced us to the sheer spiritual power and passion of great art, and liberated us from the limiting baseness of that depressing environment. Since then I've been to see any number of collections and exhibitions, many of them opened by celebrity names and accompanied by critical fanfare and acclaim, but none has shown the raw, untaught artistic genius, the intuitive mastery, that we found on the walls of a dingy backstreet attic in the poorest quarter of town.

How am I to describe the quality and the effect of the paintings we saw that evening? How can words express their visual, dramatic and intellectual charge? The first surprise was their number, nine in all, which represented tireless effort by the artist, and much burning of the midnight oil. Then there was the fact that all of them were on canvas. We had unconsciously been expecting most, if not all, to be on hardboard for reasons of economy, but Tony must have spent every penny he had on canvas and stretchers, a sacrifice to his creative urge.

These were just initial, superficial responses, however. It was the paintings themselves that demanded, compelled, full attention. One of our tutors had told us that art should engage the viewer; these paintings engrossed us, enslaved us, enthralled us. As the Streetlight title implied, they were city scenes at night, and the backgrounds, deftly suggested by strong, economical brushwork, were those of shadowy pavements, rundown shops and deep alleyways. Splashes of light from street lamps and shaded windows partly illuminated the dark corners to produce a chiaroscuro effect, but although the buildings and streets seemed at first sight to be painted in a kind of monochrome, grisaille style, closer inspection revealed the subtlest hints of yellow and ochre and olive in the light and dark and grey masses. Overall the impression was of a drab, uninviting, and slightly sinister mise en scene.

Against these inner city backdrops the artist had depicted a series of nine scenes, catching and freezing a moment of human contact or connection. In each case a young woman was involved in some common transaction or communication with a man. From a distance there seemed nothing extraordinary in these little vignettes, but the composition of the pictures and the fall of the lighting drew the eye irresistibly to the faces of the two figures, and the paintings' mesmerism had begun. Those facial expressions are as firmly ingrained in my mind's eye right now as they were just after I had first seen them, and they are still just as intriguing, disturbing, absorbing. I can recall all of them, but I will try to describe three which I feel are fairly representative.

The first picture, STREET ANGEL, ostensibly portrayed a little moment of casual kindness. A pretty young woman, dressed in black, is just on the point of dropping a coin into a cap on the pavement. The cap's owner is a beggar sitting with his back against a tree growing from the cracked flagstone, an arm drooped over a bent knee, the other leg stretched out directly in the path of the woman. Something is wrong, however. It is not just the oddity of the tree growing from the paving, or the beggar choosing to rest against the tree instead of the adjacent wall.

The faces! Where is the kindness in the girl's expression, where the gratitude in the man's? Behind the prettiness in the young woman's countenance is something else, something in the eyes, the curve of the mouth, the turn of the head. There is a cunning, an artfulness, even a hint of cruelty. Nor is the beggar some grizzled derelict. He is young and virile and would be handsome were there not in his raised face a goatish lust, together with a malice, a hatred.

Is the coin a donation, or is it a payment, a bribe? Has he barred the way of the woman or has she cornered and subdued him? And the Tree? And which figure is the Angel? Will she trip on the outstretched leg? Fallen angel? Angel in black?

I remember this was the first of Tony's paintings I came to in the gallery and not only was I overwhelmed by the ambivalence of its subject, I was amazed by the skill and technique of the artwork and the command of tone and colour. Reflected neon light from the wet street threw a kind of garish, lurid hue on the faces, a red and greenish tinge that further compromised the potential for humanity in the scene and characters.

The second picture, THE DEAL, was an indoor one set in a pawnshop. The shapes of various items on the shelves and behind the old-fashioned wooden counter were vaguely discernible in the light coming through the dusty shop window from a street lamp.

Once more a young woman, slim and fragile, was at the centre of the composition. The man behind the counter was huge, gross, with a froglike throat and bulging eyes. His bloated stomach seemed to swell out over the counter for support. What was puzzling in the action of the scene was that there was no evidence of any item being presented, pawned; instead, the girl was reaching money across the counter to the fat man.

Once more the faces defied the usual. The man's batrachian features, where greed or lasciviousness might have been expected, showed a kind of fear unsuccessfully hidden by a smirk. As for the woman, there was a knowingness in her expression that was as baffling as the famous Mona Lisa smile. What could the deal be between these two? Why was he receiving money over his pawnshop counter, and who was profiting from whatever transaction was happening? What was the relationship between the attractive young woman and the repellent amphibian pawnbroker?

I think this painting disturbed me more than any of the others, even though I again marvelled at the perfection of the artistry. Blackmail, prostitution, and darker taboo subjects like incest and paedophilia flooded my thoughts as I stood transfixed before the canvas. I remember Gareth commenting on the grotesque toad man and joking that it was more a pondshop than a pawnshop. I think he needed the feeble remark to steady himself.

I suppose if a pedant wanted to find fault with Tony's exhibition he could have pointed out that there was a sameness of scene and subject in them all, that the theme restricted the scope of the work. True, but I would have countered that greatness is not in width, but depth. THE TRYST, the last painting I will try to describe, was indeed similar in background and content. Its romantic title for me was a word that always had connotations of lovers' secret rendezvous meetings and elopements, pastoral assignations and daring runaway adventures, so I found its application to a city street scene immediately incongruous. The painting itself reinforced that sense of incompatibility. The lovers' meeting place was a dark alley between two tall terrace houses. The girl in her dark attire merged so completely into the blackness that only her pale face and thin hands would have stood out had a streetlight in the middle distance not backlit her hair and fringed it with a grayish rim. The man, who had his left arm round her thin shoulder, was caught just at the moment of withdrawing some small object from his pocket. Those arguing the case for a ring, or tickets to some getaway place, would have found it hard to explain the expressions on the two faces. In her wan smile was written a desperate need, an anguish tempered by hope and relief, while her lover, if such he were, revealed a bizarre blend of affection, pity and contempt in his furtive sideways glance.

Gareth and I studied this painting together in silence. There was more humanity inherent in it than in any of the other eight. The compassion conveyed by the artist held us spellbound. This was more than a backstreet drug deal. The nature of the relationship was much more complex, elusive, than that between supplier and user.

Elusive. There was that word again, and it suddenly struck me that what Tony may have been sublimating in his art was his own personal inscrutability and ambivalence. His work, a depiction of the contemporary urban world around him, could have been a reflection of his inner self, and possibly an unconscious attempt to understand himself.

Nine paintings in a small top floor room, and it took Gareth and me over an hour to view them. We had no awareness of the passing of time. Finally Tony joined us. He had kept a discreet distance throughout our viewing. The flush on his face suggested he had been fortifying himself against the cold with the help of the deep red wine. We congratulated him effusively on his work, but both Gareth and I found it difficult to convey our admiration adequately. Superlatives soon begin to sound hollow, even when they are spoken in full sincerity.

Tony accepted our praise quietly. He seemed preoccupied or uncertain until, as though he had reached a decision, he asked us for a favour.

"Could you please tell people in College about the exhibition? I don't want you to recommend it, but just let them know it's on, and where. Maybe you could hand out a few flyers for me? I've invited my two tutors tomorrow afternoon, and they might look more kindly on it if there are a few others here. I'm hoping for a stay of execution."

Gareth drove me home through the cold, empty streets. We were both silent. I was marvelling at the skill needed to portray such a range of conflicting, contradictory emotions in the human face. I've never seen it matched in the work of any other artist, before or since.

Just as Gareth was dropping me off he suddenly said, "The crown jewels in a cigar box." It was the sharpest remark I ever heard him make.

The events of the following day are so punctuated with question marks that I have never been able to resolve them satisfactorily in my mind. Gareth and I, not because we had been requested to do so, spent the morning spreading the word to everyone we met in College, not just the First Year students, urging them to visit the Art Exhibition of a lifetime, unlike anything they had seen before in books, galleries, or museums. In general the response was one of interest, or perhaps curiosity is more accurate, but there were too, of course, traces of scepticism, jealousy, and resentment.

About eleven o'clock, and I've never been able to find out exactly how, the terrible news reached the College: an overnight fire in Sugar Lane had completely destroyed the building housing Tony's makeshift gallery. Everything was lost. There was no information about anyone being injured in the blaze.

At first Gareth and I thought the story was a student joke in response to our promotional campaign, but when we realised there was no such intention we were totally staggered, stunned. We simply couldn't believe that the building, the gallery, and, above all, the paintings, were no more. We had to see for ourselves. Gareth drove down there in a grim silence very unlike the rapt one of the previous evening. Tabard Street was closed off when we arrived, but we parked nearby and were able to walk down its narrow thoroughfare. Even before we reached the Sugar Lane alley we could smell the sooty reek of burnt timber.

The whole building was gone, leaving a black smouldering gap, locals standing staring at the ruins in shocked disbelief. Apparently the fire had taken such a hold by the time the fire engines got there that the firemen abandoned any hope of saving the property and concentrated their efforts on stopping the flames spreading to the adjoining premises. We asked the onlookers if they had seen Tony or the girls, giving their descriptions, but they seemed too confused to be sure about anything. One of the engines was still at the scene to douse any glowing embers. I asked the nearest fireman if there had been any casualties.

"No, sir, no loss of life, that's the main thing. These old buildings are full of pitch pine, dry as tinder. It's a pity more of them aren't up in flames. It would save the bulldozers. They're worth nothing and there's nothing of any value in them……."

When we got back to College the news had spread as quickly as the fire itself. We were in the Common Room. A smart-ass was making capital out of the situation, exploiting poor Tony's appalling misfortune for cheap laughs. He was waving about one of the flyers we had distributed earlier.

"Streetlight? He shoulda called it Street Lit. It was a red hot success, a blaze of glory."

I never thought Gareth could move so fast, but in an instant he was in front of the joker and punched him full in the face, sending him sprawling and clutching a bloody nose. It was, without doubt, Gareth's finest hour.

In the days that followed all kinds of rumours circulated about the fire: Tony himself had started it out of disappointment; the owner had started it for the insurance; Greaves and Halliday had started it out of artistic jealousy; one of Tony's harem of pale young women had started it out of sexual jealousy. And so it raged for a time until, like all such incidents, it faded from popular currency. My own feeling, and it is nothing stronger than that, a feeling based on no hard evidence, is that the fire had most likely been started, accidentally or otherwise, by the two derelicts who were probably using the gallery as a shelter for the night.

As for Tony himself, the rumours were even more fanciful, more colourful: he had burned to death in the fire, and his body had been totally consumed; he was in prison on drugs charges; he was running a brothel with the pale young women; the paintings were not his but had been stolen and he was on the run from dangerous art criminals; he had jumped off a bridge in despair at the failure of his exhibition.

We never saw him again, never heard of him again. He disappeared, this time for good. I suppose, on reflection, any other outcome would have been unsuitable for Tony Graham, someone who flickered brightly in our lives for a brief spell but someone whose presence was ephemeral and whose talents were both sublime and subliminal. The only comfort Gareth and I could take from the sad sequence of events that took Tony away from us was that we were among only a very small, select and fortunate handful who got to see the brilliance of his artistic genius.

What about the other two members of the gang of three, or two and a fraction, as Tony used to call us? Amazingly, yet predictably, Gareth stayed the course and by dint of dogged determination and force of will obtained his degree. The last I saw of him he was a Schools Inspector of Art. As Tony had once remarked in The Eager Elbow, "If you can't do it, teach it, and if you can't teach it, inspect it."

I never did graduate from Art College. I quit at the end of the first year. Having seen Tony's work, I knew I was there under false pretences. I became a writer, short stories mostly, and a novel or two. Was I any good? Hard to say. I guess I'm still trying to make my mark.